Crossing Rivers

Skeeter Wilson

Thank you for staying at Our Treehouse.

I hope you enjoy these Stories about My Africa

Skeet

TO JACQUE

The joy in my life

CONTENTS

ACKNOWLEDGMENTS

Dr. Samuel Waweru, a professor at Kenyatta University, who arranged most of the interviews during my field study of the Gikuyu people in Kenya. For his knowledge of the Gikuyu culture and patience with my endless questions, I am grateful.

Mzee Oscar Chege, a good friend from my birthplace in Kenya, provided a place for me to stay and write, and he arranged several additional interviews with delightful and wise elderly Gikuyu men and women.

Dr. Kiarie Njoroge, a professor at Nairobi's Catholic University, provided valuable insight on the original Gikuyu belief system. He is a brilliant man, and I am honored to have met him and to have been, for a short time, his student.

Mzee William Giuthumo, an elder who lived near my childhood home. He proved to be a valuable resource for his sophisticated understanding of Gikuyu culture, clan relationships, land boundaries, community structure, cultural dances, and the trading relationships between the Maasai and the Gikuyu.

Mzee Ignatius Gacheru focused our discussions on the nature of marriage relationships and the philosophical basis of Gikuyu culture. He provided insight into misconceptions that *wazungu* (white people) tenaciously hold onto about the Gikuyu.

I am indebted to the many other elderly men and women who provided insight, verified information, and filled in many gaps in my understanding of the Gikuyu.

Most of all, I am deeply grateful to Mzee John Mouitherero, who agreed to interviews under the mango tree in his shamba (farm). His stories about his mother's life are the inspiration for this novel and several sequels to follow. I am honored that I was allowed to hear this story and that Mzee Mouitherero has allowed me to base this novel on his mother's life.

PREFACE

I was born in Kenya among the Gikuyu people. My coming-of-age experiences were set against the backdrop of their customs and culture. While seeking my post-graduate degree in creative writing and African history, I conducted a field study in Kenya that focused on interviews with elderly Gikuyu, both men and women. My research was focused on what the life and the culture of the people I grew up with was like before colonialism.

I was privileged, during my field study in Kenya, to interview a 102-year-old Gikuyu elder who recounted the story of his mother. Her life began in the 1880s, before colonialism. She was witness to the radical changes that took place when the first "white people" showed up, and she lived long enough to watch her sons struggle to maintain their land rights under colonial law. She saw one of her sons fight with the British in WW2, and then both of her sons were on opposite sides during the Mau Mau wars. She lived to see her sons reconciled before her death in the early 1970s. I realized that this remarkable woman's story should be told. I asked the elder for permission to write a novel based on his mother's life. He agreed.

Crossing Rivers is the first of several books in a series intended to span the length of her life. The story begins in the 1880s, just before British colonialism.

Details of the story are mine based on my experience, research, and imagination as a writer. While generally based on a real life, this is fiction. All mistakes and misrepresentations of the Gikuyu people are mine.

I am not a spokesperson for the Gikuyu people. Neither do I claim to be providing a complete picture of this rich and complex culture. The Gikuyu people have very capable historians and writers. They can and do speak for themselves.

I was, however, born among the Gikuyu people, and this story is my tribute to them and their fascinating history. It is my way of thanking them for being among the first teachers in my journey of life.

Skeeter Wilson

SECOND EDITION PREFACE

I am humbled by the response to this story both by the western and African audience that it has found. Story-telling is very different in the African cultures among whom I grew up than most western readers are accustomed to. The different styles can be a little jarring. I hoped that I might be able to bridge the gap and give both audiences enough of what they expect in a story so that both would approve. It seems this has been the case.

Of course, my Gikuyu readers, were very quick to point out a variety of little mistakes that they noticed in my story telling. For instance, I used the word "dirt" when talking about a burial. The objection is that the Gikuyu never burry in dirt; they burry in soil. In the American lexicon the nuance may be slight, but for them this is rather important. In another section, I had Gikuyu elders drinking from a reed straw. I felt I had researched their method adequately to describe this action. However, it was pointed out to me, and I later was able to verify, the Gikuyu never used reed straws, but instead they used decorated cow horns to drink their beer. A final example, and probably my biggest error, was the misspelling of the name Wangari. In the first edition I spelled it "Wangai," which is decidedly a male name, instead of "Wangari," which is the female name. In this edition these errors are addressed. While to the western audience these may have gone unnoticed, they are, I believe, important corrections to make for my Agikuyu audience.

The fact that Gikuyu people sought to point out these mistakes, rather than dismiss my work, is a great honor. I am always open to additional corrections in the event a future edition is published.

Skeeter Wilson

THE RIVER

Ma'muriuki shuddered as she dipped her toe into the muddy water at the river's edge. It seemed like the best place to cross, but with the rains the night before, she did not know how deep it would be toward the middle, where the water was moving the fastest. She glanced back the way they had come. She did not see anyone, but she would not feel safe until the river was between her and the village. Her focus moved to her oldest daughter, Wangari, a few steps back. The young girl looked behind her and then into her mother's eyes. A flicker of fear showed in her face.

"Wait here, child. I will be back for you," she called to Wangari. She tightened the *ngoi* binding that wrapped her youngest child, Maathai, on her back. He whimpered, sensing his mother's concern. "Wangari, child, answer me when I call to you. Do you understand?"

"Yes, Mama," Wangari said. "I will wait for you." Wangari's eyes darted between her mother and the trail behind her. "Hurry, Mama."

"Good, child," Ma'muriuki said. She picked up her second daughter, Makena, and placed the wiggling little girl on her hip. "Still, child," she said, slapping the little girl's thigh sharply. Makena settled down immediately, and the young mother stepped into the river that had swollen overnight in the downpour. She could not go back now. She hoped to find shelter before nightfall in one of the homes of the clan that lived across the river.

She shuddered again in the cold water and then ignored it. Finding stable footholds on jagged rocks, she worked toward the roiling middle, where the rocks were smoother and more slippery. She fought against the water urging her downstream. Makena squealed suddenly as her foot hit the cold water, startling Ma'muriuki. For a few precarious moments she struggled to regain her balance. "Still, child," she warned, muted by the rushing water. She shifted Makena higher on her hip and plunged to her waist with the next step. Makena shuddered quietly against the shock of cold water. Maathai whimpered as his tiny legs dipped into the river.

Ma'muriuki took a step but could not find the bottom. She slipped and sent them tumbling under the brown froth. She slammed her hip against a large rock and braced against it, struggling to her feet. The heads of her children broke out of the water, rigid with panic. They gasped for air and wailed above the water's roar.

Ma'muriuki pulled them to calmer waters and dry land. She set her children on the grass and briskly rubbed warmth into their nearly naked bodies. She took off her *shuka* and laid it out in the afternoon sun, wincing at the pain in her hip. She looked down at the bloody gash in her side.

"Mama!" Makena screamed.

She whirled around. Makena pointed to the river, to Wangari being swept downstream. Her older daughter disappeared around the corner.

"Hold Maathai, my daughter, but do not follow me!" Ma'muriuki shouted. She ran naked down the side of the river, breathing a prayer to Ngai, fighting the creeping doubt that Ngai would even listen to her now. She leapt over a patch of whistling thorn bushes without a second thought and landed hard on her heels. A sharp pain shot through her foot as she sped around the corner, trying to catch a glimpse of her daughter.

A dark form bobbed in the middle of the river. Ma'muriuki first thought it was a branch caught in the rocks and then realized it was Wangari. The young girl's listless body surfaced briefly before plunging back under the water. Ma'muriuki jumped in after her, and as the young girl surfaced again, she screamed for her daughter. The current pulled her under, but she was more determined than the water's rage. She caught a boulder and pulled herself to the surface again. Leaning into the current, she grabbed the limp body and felt down to the girl's foot, caught between two rocks. She wrapped her arms around her daughter and pushed her back against the river's flow until the foot came loose. The water's force hurled them down the river another twenty feet until Ma'muriuki grabbed the branch of a fallen tree and pulled the two of them to the shore.

Terrified, Ma'muriuki lifted Wangari into her arms and ran back to her other children. With one step, she begged Ngai to give her child back to her, and with the next, she begged Wangari to come back.

She laid her daughter next to Maathai and Makena, both shivering on the spot where she had left them. She moved them on top of Wangari and wrapped her still-wet shuka around the three children in the hope that their body warmth would revive her daughter.

Ma'muriuki struggled to remember some herb or plant that might aid in bringing Wangari back to her, but the only thing that struck her was warmth. Wangari needed more warmth. She felt the early shadows of approaching darkness and realized it was too late to look for a house. They would have to spend the night there. She had wanted to get further away from the river, but it was too late for that too. She looked around and decided they were hidden enough to not be seen easily from the other side of the river.

She set about making a fire to survive the night. It would have to be a hot fire with very dry wood to reduce the smoke. She walked on the side of her foot to avoid stepping on the thorn lodged in her sole, but the pain was beginning to distract her. Hobbling along, she quickly found some dry moss, leaves, and sticks, and then looked around for a thin hardwood branch to make a fire stick. She broke off a branch and picked up two large, flat river rocks and three small, round stones and then returned to her children. With each step, her stride gave way to the pain in her foot.

"Mama!"

At the call, Ma'muriuki picked up her pace and found Wangari up on one elbow next to her sister as Maathai lay sleeping between them. The mother quickly embraced her oldest daughter and held her in grateful silence. Then she cupped her daughter's face in her hands and looked into her eyes. Both mother and daughter wore the tracks of tears on their faces.

"Ngai has returned you to us, my child. We will offer thanks," Ma'muriuki said.

Wangari offered a faint smile with ashen gray lips and bloodshot eyes.

"Don't speak, child. Rest, and I will make a fire. My *thoroko* and *njahi* have become wet. I will cook them for you so they will not spoil." She took the small, sodden bag of mixed peas and beans from around her neck and laid them on the ground. She then hit a large rock along the edge of a smaller rock with all her might, leaving a sharp, jagged edge to sharpen a point on the fire stick. After digging a small indentation into a log, she placed pieces of dried moss over the notch and pierced through the moss with the fire stick until it fit neatly inside. She spun the stick vigorously as she rubbed it between her hands, slowly working them to the bottom and returning to the top and starting again. A wisp of smoke arose and then another and then Ma'muriuki leaned over, still rotating the sticks, and blew on the moss. At the first flare of fire, she added more moss and dried leaves, blowing steadily at the base of the flames. She added sticks until she grunted her satisfaction and dropped the three small stones into the hottest part of the fire. She then took her wet shuka from around her children and laid it out next to the fire to dry.

It was time to tend to her foot. She glanced briefly at the end of the four-inch thorn that had pierced through the ball of her foot and broken the skin near the toes. She had unknown days of walking ahead and needed to remove the thorn quickly.

She winced at the pain as she wiggled the spine. She could not risk breaking the thorn inside her foot, so she wiggled and twisted it methodically. When she could not endure the pain any longer, she stood and hobbled to the river and sat with her foot in the cold water until it went numb. She continued working on the thorn, occasionally plunging her foot back into the water. Finally, she felt the spine give a little. She soaked her foot once more and then grabbed the bottom of the thorn and pulled it straight out in one swift jerk. She could not stifle the cry that escaped her lips, but she hoped the noisy water prevented her children from hearing her agony.

She soaked her throbbing foot a few more moments. Untying a cooking gourd from around her waist, she removed its leather cap and filled it with water. Relieved at last, she walked quickly back to her children. Darkness had fallen, and she could see their flickering faces looking for her as she emerged from the shadows.

Wangari was sitting up. Ma'muriuki could see new tracks of tears on her face in the firelight. "Mama, I am sorry I did not wait for you on the other side like you told me. I watched you, Maathai, and Makena fall beneath the water, and when I did not see you come up again, I decided if I did not come for you, there would be no one left. I am foolish for not listening to you. I beg you to forgive me, Mama!"

"My daughter, you are a child still, and *the foolishness of a child will end with childhood*. It is not yet time for you to carry the burdens of this world on your back. What you did was brave but foolish, and children do foolish things. There is nothing to forgive. Ngai has given you back to me, and when one receives such a gift from the one who creates all things, there is no room left for anger at the loving foolishness of a child. Now wait for me, and I will prepare some food."

Ma'muriuki stood up. "Now, children, learn from this. *Ngai is not to be bothered by small things but rather to be praised.* For, it is true that *there is no one who forgets Ngai in their troubles.*" She emptied half the water from the gourd onto the ground. She lifted her hands and began to pray. "Ngai, creator of all things, my child, Wangari, was with you in your place before she was born, but in your mercy and kindness to me, you blessed me by giving her to my care for her time on earth. You can take her to be with you at any time, for she belongs to you. But you listened to a mother's tears, and you have given her back to me again. For this, my heart is grateful. I beg that the evening of life will come to me before it comes to the children you have blessed me with. It is always a mother's desire to close her eyes before the eyes of her children are closed. But you alone are the creator."

Dropping her hands, Ma'muriuki sat down and put the peas and beans into the gourd. Using two sticks, she took one of the round stones out of the fire and placed it into the gourd as well. Steam rushed out of the top. She picked up the second stone with the sticks and then the third, dropping both into the gourd. When the water reached a boiling frenzy, she mashed the peas into the water with a stick until they reached the consistency she wanted.

Ma'muriuki poured the contents over the flat surface of the larger river rock and fed her children a small portion at a time, and then took a portion for herself. It was not enough for a regular meal, but it would hold them until the next day. She was not far from the trading route, where she would find more food.

The children quietly watched their mother. Wangari had been in the world for eight complete seasons. Her thin body rippled with the strength of a child who spent her days digging up weeds in the *shamba*, pounding grain into flour, and helping her mother take care of her younger siblings.

She'd had one hole in the upper lobe of her left ear for almost a full season. The hole was a source of pride for her, because it meant her mother felt her mature enough to become a full Gikuyu in five more complete seasons. Each season would be marked by another hole in her ear. Wangari wore a small brown goatskin cloth tied around her waist and a half shuka with a faint hint of red dye tied over one shoulder and draped over her middle. She was always full of questions, and her mother showed great pride in her because of it. There was no conversation or question that Wangari could not initiate or ask, as long as she addressed her mother properly. Few things mattered more in the raising of a child than proper respect for and deference to their elders. Beyond deference to Ngai, no other respect and love was demanded more than toward one's own mother.

Makena had only lived for four full seasons. She was a quiet child. There was no expectation on her yet, except that she show respect. Her life was divided between imitating her older sister, taking care of her little brother, and playing quietly by herself. Her time to ask questions would come, but there was no hurry.

Baby Maathai had not yet lived a full season. His days were usually spent wrapped in his *ngoi* on the back of his mother or Wangari. When he was not on their backs, he would lay along the side of the shamba, giggling at the playful antics of Makena. Back in the huts, his suckling was shared by his mother and her co-wife.

"Mama." Wangari seemed deep in thought.

"Yes, child."

"Mama, I don't remember being with Ngai before I was with you."

Her mother smiled. Wangari and all her questions reminded Ma'muriuki of herself as a young girl.

"Ah, my child, none of us remember those times. Some of the medicine men do remember with fleeting images, but Ngai will give us those memories again when we return to be with the ancestors under the mugumo tree."

"Will Ngai be under the mugumo tree, too?"

"Ngai is everywhere, my child, but he gives our ancestors rest under the mugumo tree, and he visits there often. We were made by Ngai to enjoy and take care of the earth and to have many feasts and celebrations. Ngai is a father who owns the land and a mother who gives life. We are the children."

"Mama, is our father with Ngai under the mugumo tree?" Wangari asked.

Makena reached out and took her big sister's hand. She rarely spoke but with this gesture let Ma'muriuki know when she wanted to know the answer to Wangari's questions.

"Yes, my child, Ngai brings us all to the roots of the mugumo tree when it is time for us to leave this earth and return to him."

"Does our father see us from the underworld?"

"There will be times when he visits us. It is good to follow the instructions of Ngai; otherwise, one of the ancestors may visit us with curses rather than blessings."

"Will our father put curses on those who harm us too?"

"Child, it is not the way of Ngai that we should wish harm to others. We are instructed to obey him. Leave curses for the ancestors and those who do not fear Ngai."

Ma'muriuki felt her shuka. It was dry. She helped her children curl up together near the heat of the fire and covered them with the cloth.

"Mama," Wangari asked, "is Ngai an ostrich?"

Ma'muriuki laughed. "Who taught you to ask so many questions, child?"

"You taught me, Mama."

She smiled. "No, child, Ngai is not an ostrich."

"But Mama, why do people say that Ngai is an ostrich?"

"Child, why do the Gikuyu call the ostrich 'the shining one?'"

"Because of its white feathers that shine like a light in the distance."

"Yes, child," Ma'muriuki said. "Now tell me why we sometimes also call the Kirinyaga, where Ngai comes to visit,

8

an ostrich as well."

"Because of the cold white powder on the mountain that also shines like a light in the distance."

"Yes, child. Now tell me, what does shining whiteness mean to a Gikuyu?"

"It means pureness and holiness, Mama," Wangari said. "That is what you have told us."

"That, my child, is why we sometimes say Ngai is an ostrich, and at other times we call Kirinyaga the 'Mountain of Ngai.' It is not because Ngai is an ostrich or a mountain, but because Ngai is pure and holy."

"But Mama…"

"Hush, child. It is time to sleep. Save your questions for the sun."

Ma'muriuki smiled at her two girls as they lay down by the sleeping Maathai. She looked at her baby son and wondered if he would ever see his big brother Muriuki again.

A mother received her name of honor from her firstborn child. She wondered if the people she met along the way would call her Ma'wangari instead of Ma'muriuki because they would not know she had an older son. Thoughts of Muriuki sent a wave of sadness over her heart. He was still young, but he was strong and had taken care of his mother and siblings as best he could. She so desperately needed him with her on this journey, but that was beyond her control. Her heart was heavy.

Ma'muriuki watched her children fall asleep. They had never slept a night of their young lives outside the safety of their home, which was surrounded by thick thorn fences and guarded by warriors. They had never been in the woods except on occasion with the older boys, when they would help move livestock from one field to another. Her girls had learned few skills beyond cooking food and cultivating the millet, peas, and beans in the shamba. And it had been years since she had slept under the sky. The stars were easier to see when she was a child. There were not as many trees and clouds overhead to block her view.

She moved next to her children and felt a sharp jolt of pain in her back. It was the first time since crossing the river that she was reminded about her last beating. She curled up behind her children, offering her wounded back as protection against the darkness.

She listened to the drone of insects and frogs and the manic whoop of hyenas in the distance. She did not fear the lion in the thick woods that surrounded them, but she knew the eyes of the leopard were never far away. Ma'muriuki was just a little older than Wangari when she had last slept outside of the protection of a Gikuyu family house. She felt along the dark ground for some sticks. She could no longer remember which kind of wood they should be, but she hoped the hand of Ngai would direct her. She gathered a handful of thin sticks, broke them into pieces, and placed a small stick between each toe. Her first mother had told her that the sticks provided a defense against animals and bad spirits. She fell asleep trying to remember her mother's prayer, her mother's face.

MAASAI GIRL

Her first mother called her Kiserian because she was a peaceful baby. As a young girl, she helped milk the cows, listening carefully as her mother showed her how to check for disease and wounds in the cattle and goats. After the milking and inspections, her mother would signal to her brothers, who drove the cattle out of the enclosed *manyatta* to graze in the grasslands. She would then help her mother set the milk-filled gourds in the sun and drop smoldering charcoal into each one to hasten the curdling process.

She would often sit with her mother on the flat, mud-and-dung roof of the *enkaji*, smearing on a mixture of twigs, soil, and cow dung to patch holes created by the rains. On the days when it was her mother's turn, she would help repair the roof of her father's enkaji as well. She knew her mother was her father's favorite wife because he always complained that his other wives did not repair the roof as well as she did.

Her mother was also a favorite of many of her father's fellow *moran* warriors. When they would come to her house and plant their spears at the entrance, it was rare that she did not welcome them to her bed. Despite her mother's many lovers, Kiserian had only two brothers and no sisters.

The uncircumcised boys would tell Kiserian she was as

beautiful as her mother and that when she was circumcised, they wanted to be among her lovers. At times, she would let the boys play with her and even let a few try to penetrate her. She would laugh at their frustrated attempts, but between their embarrassed smiles, they said that when their strength came in, they would be back. Sometimes even the morani would pay her compliments and tell her to grow up more quickly, but they would not touch her until she became a woman.

But those days were becoming memories to her. In the last few seasons, her world had changed. Every day, the gaunt figures of her brothers returned fewer cows into the *kraal* than they had taken out that morning. Every day, Kiserian and her mother separated out more cattle that were too sick to live another day. Their skins were stretched on the outside walls of the houses to dry, to be sold to the Gikuyu traders in exchange for food. So many cattle did not make it back anymore.

Her father no longer sat up when her mother came to tell him the condition of the herd. His thin body, once so strong and fit for battle, lay on the ground outside of his enkaji, covered by a single skin of a once-prized bull. He kept his spear by his side, but Kiserian knew he was too weak to stand.

He barked angry orders at her mother as he listened to her report on what remained of his wasting cattle. She patiently continued speaking despite his outbursts. She was the only wife still living. He was not angry with Kiserian's mother—he was scared. A Maasai who could not take care of his cattle was not worthy to be a Maasai. But the cattle were dying everywhere, and along with them, the Maasai people. The famine was lasting too long. The cattle's disease raged on despite the best Maasai medicines, and the sacrifices of the medicine men went unheeded.

She watched her father and mother talk late into the night with the few remaining adult survivors. Their voices vacillated between loud and animated to quiet murmurs as they sent fugitive glances to where Kiserian sat silently in the distance. The stench of death was all around. The sound of hyenas feasting on the corpses of Maasai and livestock outside the manyatta filled the night air—a sound she had heard every night for months. She fell asleep hungry, but everyone was hungry. She did not complain because she was Maasai.

Her mother woke her early and gave her a small gourd of milk boiled with bitter herbs to keep the feeling of hunger under control.

"My daughter, we will take some cows to meet the Gikuyu traders."

Kiserian liked going to see the traders. Her mother would usually trade skins and cows for spears for her father or the other moran warriors. Recently, however, she traded only for yams, millet, and sorghum. Kiserian never liked Gikuyu food. It made her stomach hurt and growl. The Maasai complained that it was food for cows, not people. But without the Gikuyu food, many more Maasai would have died already. Kiserian was looking forward to the feeling of a complaining stomach full of food.

"Mama, we are taking all of my father's good cows to the Gikuyu. We are leaving none behind that are healthy." Kiserian knew better than to question her mother's actions. Her observation was as close to a question as a child dared venture.

"Yes, my child," her mother stated. That was all the answer Kiserian was going to get. "Before we go any further, go back to your father. He has words to speak to you."

Kiserian walked back and knelt next to her father's slumped figure. She offered him a gourd of milk mixed with blood and bitter roots. He faintly motioned the gourd away.

"My child, Enkai is the great god of the Maasai, but he has two faces. Enkai gave us all the cattle on earth to sustain us. But there are times when the kind face of Narok becomes the cruel face of Nanyoki and is vengeful on the Maasai whom he loves. For years now, our god has shown us only the anger of Nanyoki. Our *laibon* have offered sacrifices of cattle and sheep to appease his anger, and they have petitioned him to turn the face of Nanyoki away and return the kind face of Narok to us once again. But instead, Nanyoki gives our cattle and our people as gifts to the hyenas."

Kiserian sat quietly. There were no words between a daughter and her father. She already understood who Enkai was. She had learned at the knee of her mother all the things that were necessary to know about his two faces. She was well acquainted with the angry face of Nanyoki. She waited to see if her father had finished.

"My child, the Gikuyu are a strange people. They work very hard from morning to night, and the backs of their women labor under the load of heavy food that they pull from the earth. Their god, Ngai, has not been angry with the Gikuyu like Enkai has been with us. For the Maasai, the food of the Gikuyu is fit only for cattle. However, they are well fed, and their children do not go hungry at night. Perhaps Ngai of the Gikuyu is stronger than Enkai. Perhaps they are the same god, who has chosen to show kindness to the Gikuyu and anger toward the Maasai. I do not know these things. My child, you should know that there is no shame in living among the Gikuyu and taking a Gikuyu name. I have one word of instruction for you, my daughter; you must do as I say."

Kiserian tilted her head slightly to let her father know she would obey him.

"My child, on this journey, listen to your mother and do not refuse her or her instructions."

Kiserian did not understand her father's words. He motioned her to leave him and rejoin her mother. She saw the straggling remains of adults in the manyatta looking at her from their houses. Their eyes told her that everything had changed.

Her mother walked ahead, leaving Kiserian with the task of prodding the cattle along. This was the way it should be. It was a mother's task to build the shelters for the family, dig for roots, and tend to the sick animals, but it was the task of the children to move the cattle to grazing lands and to meet the Gikuyu. Usually, other young children were brought along to help bring back the heavy Gikuyu foods, but this time it was just Kiserian and her mother. Gikuyu women carried food on their backs, but a Maasai woman would not carry burdens that belonged to an animal.

"Mama, it will be a heavy task to bring back the food from all these cattle."

"We will purchase donkeys for the food," her mother said. Kiserian wrinkled her nose at the thought of donkeys, disgusting animals with little use other than carrying the frames of the huts when the manyatta moved to better grazing lands. Donkeys did not add to the wealth or status of the father. The Gikuyu seemed to have no pride in their women or their animals.

The sun was high and the sweltering heat slowed the progress of the cattle across the grasslands. Three jackals followed closely behind them, and further back slunk two hyenas, all waiting for the first victims among the cattle.

"Go away!" Kiserian shouted. "Today the cattle are strong and your bellies will not be filled." The jackals sat on their haunches, their silver backs glistening in the sun. They waited until she turned to continue their vigil behind her.

By late afternoon, the little girl and her mother saw the tops of the tall acacia trees where the Gikuyu would be waiting. It was a strategic spot, about a day's journey from several Maasai manyattas. The pale yellow bark and dark green leaves stood in stark contrast to the dirty yellow savannah lands. Kiserian waved at her mother and pointed to the trees. Her mother nodded slightly.

Before they reached their destination, Kiserian's mother signaled to her. The young girl circled the cattle, pulling up thorn bushes by the roots and stacking them around the herd, leaving two small openings. Her mother built fires from other thorn bushes and placed them in front of the openings. Negotiations would begin in the morning. No Maasai wanted to spend the night in the same camp as the Gikuyu. Mother and daughter sat listening as the night air filled with the calls of hyenas and jackals and the distant grunts of lions.

The lions' roars grew louder. The cattle got to their feet, their wide eyes reflecting the firelight. Kiserian's mother stood up and walked outside of the fenced encampment. She brought back long green sticks and broke them into small lengths. She placed a small stick between each toe and handed the rest to her daughter to do the same.

She lifted her hands above her head. "Enkai, hear my voice. I am your daughter and I can neither breathe nor speak unless you give me breath. I call upon your protection tonight. We do not fear the lion because you alone can open and shut the mouth of the lion. We call upon you to protect us against the spirits of those who would do us evil and against the lion who would do us harm."

With that, Kiserian's mother lay down and fell asleep. Her daughter curled up beside her.

At first light, they approached the Gikuyu women sitting next to their heavy baskets, waiting. As the girl and mother neared, they could hear the women's chatter. Kiserian found the Gikuyu language repulsive, but the leader of the women, and sometimes others, always spoke Maasai. Her mother had told her these women had once been Maasai. Kiserian found this abhorrent. Why would a woman leave the Maasai and become a beast of burden for the Gikuyu?

The women stood up at the arrival of the cattle and carefully inspected them. They looked in the mouth for signs of fever and in the eyes and nose for cloudy discharge—any of these indicators and they would reject the entire herd. Kiserian and her mother had chosen carefully.

Her mother negotiated only for food. She did not inspect the spears or swords. The Gikuyu women seemed to understand the singular purpose of the visit and quickly loaded two donkeys with the food. Kiserian spotted some arrowroot and yams among the grains in one of the donkeys' baskets.

As the Gikuyu women took control of the cattle, Kiserian

spat on the ground in disgust at the sight of a woman doing the work of a child. Her mother turned and with a glance stopped her from any further displays of disrespect.

The young girl watched as her mother took the oldest woman aside. The two leaned close together in a hushed conversation until the older woman turned and called two others to join them. Then Kiserian's mother signaled her to come as well.

The young Maasai girl came and stood stoically by her mother. The Gikuyu woman grabbed her arm. "This one is skinny, probably lazy too."

Kiserian almost laughed but caught herself. She did not expect a Gikuyu woman to talk like a Maasai. She glanced into the old woman's face and was surprised by the kindness in her eyes.

"She is strong, and her spirit is stronger," Kiserian's mother said.

"Does she still have a father on this earth, or is he given to the hyenas?"

"Her father lives, but the hyenas linger close by."

"It is not proper to make this exchange without the father to give consent."

"Her father's strength is given to the earth. If he were to walk, he would belong to the hyenas before he left the manyatta where he sits."

"Does the stupid Maasai girl agree that her father's weakness is too great to walk?" the Gikuyu woman asked.

Kiserian agreed with a slight tilt of her head.

"Did your father give you any instructions before you followed your mother?"

The girl felt weak as realization of what was happening came over her. "My father told me to listen to my mother and to not refuse her or her instructions."

The old woman looked with sympathy into Kiserian's eyes for a moment and then turned to the other two Gikuyu women. "You have heard this. Now you must be witnesses to what follows, so we may tell the council."

Kiserian did not look at her mother but felt her trembling through her firm grip on her shoulder. The Gikuyu woman reached out and gently turned mother and daughter toward her and told them to follow her instructions. She bent down and broke off the tops of the grass growing around the trees. When she was satisfied, she straightened and faced them.

"We do not steal children—we do not force others to become Gikuyu. We will not take this Maasai girl to live among the Gikuyu. We have plenty of Gikuyu girls to marry our men and raise the children that Ngai gives us. We do not need more. If this lazy Maasai girl comes with us, she must be a Gikuyu. Ngai has given us our land, but he instructs us to work hard with our hands to make it a land plentiful for us and for helping others like the lazy Maasai. If she comes with us, she comes as one who will plant the seed, pull the weeds, and learn the ways of the Gikuyu without reservation. But we ask the Maasai mother to take her daughter home with the food we have given her; we do not need this girl."

Kiserian could hardly breathe as she waited for her mother to speak.

"It has been too many years since Enkai Narok has shown his face to us." Her mother's voice was determined. "We have only seen the angry face of Enkai Nanyoki. With this food, I may give my husband a few more days of life, but after that, both my children and I will soon die. It is better that I give one of my children for food. With that food, those of us who remain may survive until the anger of Enkai is over. But this child will go with the Gikuyu as you have said, because Ngai of the Gikuyu has given you a land of plenty, and this girl who was until now my daughter will have plenty. She has a strong spirit and she will be a good Gikuyu woman."

The old woman turned to the two women standing with her. "Have you heard all that was said here?"

"We have heard."

The woman put the grass in her mouth and chewed it into a green mash. She motioned for Kiserian and her mother to extend their hands and form a cup. The woman spit a large wad of grass first into her mother's hand and then into Kiserian's. She looked directly at Kiserian's mother. "It is time for you to give us instructions so that we and your daughter may know your decision."

"I give my child to you, and my instructions to her are to love and obey you. She is now born of your family and of your womb. Whether I live or die, I give only blessings and not curses to you and to her who is now your daughter."

"Have you heard all that was said here?" The old woman glanced at the other two.

"We have heard."

She turned again to Kiserian and her mother. "We will leave now. Our journey back to our lands is long. Speak what you must, and we will see if your feet are as good as your words."

Mother and child stood under the acacia trees and watched the Gikuyu women load the unbartered supplies onto their backs and the remaining donkeys. They drove the cattle out of the thicket and back onto the trail toward the Gikuyu highlands. Still, her mother stood silent. Then she sat on the ground and looked at her hands filled with chewed pulp. She let it drip through her fingers and wiped them on the grass. Kiserian sat down and followed her mother's example. They watched the slow progress of the Gikuyu traders until the women almost disappeared.

Kiserian's mother stood. She picked up Kiserian's herding stick and grabbed the sisal ropes tied around the donkeys' necks. The girl got to her feet and watched her. She had never seen her mother holding donkeys or a herding stick.

"Child, come here." Kiserian went and stood next to her. "The one who holds these donkeys will return this food to the Maasai people." She held out the herding stick to her daughter. Kiserian took the stick quietly. "The one who holds the stick is no longer a Maasai; she now belongs to the Gikuyu, who are now heading to the Gikuyu lands. The one who holds the stick will turn her back on the Maasai, and she will not look back. Those are my final words; you must remember the voice of your father."

Kiserian listened to the brays of the protesting donkeys behind her. She listened as the footsteps of the woman who had once been her mother faded into the distance. She wondered if she would ever see her face again. She tried to take a step toward the women in front of her but felt riveted to the ground. The girl gathered her strength because it was a step she knew she must take.

***

Kiserian followed the Gikuyu women at a distance, unsure of how to approach them. She slowly worked her way closer. The old women would stop from time to time and watch the little girl's progress toward them. As the midday began to simmer, the Gikuyu circled the cattle and sat under trees to let the heat of the day pass. Kiserian came to within one hundred steps of the resting Gikuyu and then sat down and waited. The old woman stood up and walked to her. Kiserian trembled in fear but collected herself. A Maasai shows no fear to a Gikuyu.

"Stupid Maasai girl, why do you follow the Gikuyu? Go home to your mother and eat the Maasai blood and milk. We have no part with lazy Maasai girls. We have a saying: *One cannot eat what another has planted.*"

Kiserian sat still, staring straight ahead as if ignoring the woman, angry that she had insulted the Maasai. She wanted to spit her disgust at seeing a former Maasai woman used as a pack animal for the Gikuyu men. But her mother's words held her in check. *You are no longer a Maasai; you are Gikuyu now.* She wondered if this was the same way this woman had become a Gikuyu.

The woman stood and walked back to the other resting women. Kiserian stared ahead at the Mountain of Boys, just a few hours' walk ahead. The Maasai said that if a boy ran around that little mountain seven times, he would become a girl. She had never been beyond the mountain but had always wondered what would happen if a girl ran around it seven times. Beyond the low peak, along the steep sides of the valley, lived the N'dorobo hunters. In the trees above the valley lay the home of the Gikuyu people. It was not a question of going back. The instructions of her mother and the voice of her father was all she needed. She must join the Gikuyu. But she did not know how.

The Gikuyu got up and moved the herd again. Kiserian jumped up and ran toward the cattle. The women were not moving them very well. She did not know how to be a Gikuyu, but she did know how to take care of cattle. She ran past the women, holding her stick above her head. She swatted a large spotted cow on the rump until it moved ahead of the others. Kiserian patted it on the face, speaking softly, and then walked in front of the cow, whistling sharply. The other cattle fell in line behind.

GIKUYU WOMEN

Ma'muriuki awoke to the rhythmic *coo-ca-coo-coo-coo* of the mourning dove. It was still dark, but she could see the early hues of dawn faintly whisking through the trees. The air was cold. She gently touched her children sleeping by the dying embers and then gathered dry sticks and branches and rekindled the fire. Her children woke to the sound of her movements and sat quietly, waiting for her to finish. As the flames crackled to life, she sat down and huddled with the children until the fire warmed them.

"We have a long walk in front of us, my children, but the journey will be good and we will not go hungry."

"Mama, will we see Muriuki again?" Makena asked.

"The day will come, my child. Ngai will not keep us apart forever. We will see him again. *Ngai will give restitution to us when others do us wrong.*" She felt uneasy making that promise because she did not have much control over the matter. But her prayers to Ngai had been strong. There was hope of seeing her oldest son again.

She inspected the bottom of her foot. There was a slight inflammation where the thorn had pierced the skin. She sent Wangari to get some yellow *ndongu* fruit and took her other children down to the river. She was washing her foot when Wangari returned with the berries.

"Do not eat these, my children, as they will give you a great sickness, but they are useful to heal wounds. *The forests hide the enemy but are full of medicine.* My wound is slight, but we have far to walk, and I will use the ndongu to make the healing go quickly." She crushed the yellow fruit in her hands and massaged her foot with the juice. She sat until the liquid dried in the sun. Then they resumed their journey.

They picked their way through the woods, following a faint path that disappeared at times under thick brush. Ma'muriuki was not concerned, as she knew they would find the main trail soon. *It is the little paths that lead to the big ones.*

They came to a hedge of thorns and sharp pointed sticks. On the other side was a cultivated shamba with banana trees and millet grass. Ma'muriuki climbed over a ladder stile and lifted her children to the cultivated side. She spotted a woman working in the field ahead and worked her way toward her carefully to avoid causing damage to the crops.

"Mama, can we eat a banana?" Makena pleaded.

"Child, you need to understand the ways of a traveler. *One who travels is one who learns.* One may eat food from the shamba of a stranger if they do not see the owner. However, if they do see the owner, they must approach them first. Do you not see that woman ahead? We will ask the way to the trading route. The choice of eating the bananas belongs to her, not to us."

The woman heard their approach and stood up. "*Mwemwega!*" Her friendly shout carried to the huts behind her, alerting her family that visitors were approaching.

"*Demwega,*" Ma'muriuki replied.

The two women clapped their right hands together high over their heads and smiled broadly. The children stood by in respectful silence as the women went through the formalities of a Gikuyu greeting. They spoke of their age group, which Gikuyu clan they came from, and their husbands. Ma'muriuki kept her answers vague and spoke only of her first husband. She identified herself as belonging to the clan of her Gikuyu parents. She said she was looking for the trading path that led to the Mountain of Boys so she could see if her Maasai mother still lived. It was as much as she was willing to tell.

The other woman looked at Ma'muriuki kindly. It was clear that something was being kept hidden in the story, but the woman did not seem to mind.

"The path you have chosen is just beyond my shamba," she said, pointing past the huts. "But for now, you will come to my home." She turned and shouted instructions to the figures emerging from the houses.

A Gikuyu homestead was composed of several buildings. In the center was the first wife's house, with a small, elevated granary in front of it. To each side of the first wife were similar houses with granaries for the second, third, and as many more as there were additional wives. Separate and to the side of the wives' houses was the husband's hut. When there were older unmarried sons, they sometimes had a small hut built behind their mother's house. The homestead was the property of the wives, and the husband was considered a guest on their property.

Motioning for Ma'muriuki and her children to follow her, the woman they met in the field led them to an older woman standing in front of the central first wife's house. After a brief introduction, she told the older woman about Ma'muriuki's age group. The first wife smiled as she slapped Ma'muriuki's hand and then pointed to another wife standing outside of her hut. "There is your age mate. She will prepare a meal, and then we will join you."

All Gikuyu who were circumcised in the same year were considered a fraternity of equals who took care of each other under any circumstance. After greeting each other, the age mate sent her children scurrying away with duties to fulfill. One child picked up Maathai and began to play with him, while another girl carried off Ma'muriuki's gourd and empty bag for beans. Her daughters were paired off with other children, who chatted with them as they ground millet and picked bananas.

"I see your foot is sick," Ma'muriuki's new friend said.

"Let me look." The young woman inspected it. "This foot needs to rest today, because the journey to the Mountain of Boys is a long one. You will stay with me until the morning."

Ma'muriuki could not refuse the kindness of an age mate and was relieved to have some time to rest her injured foot. The age mate went to the hut of the fourth wife, who came out carrying ash, yellow acacia bark, and more of the yellow ndongu fruit. She sat down beside Ma'muriuki, inspected her foot, and crushed the bark to a powder, which she then mixed into a paste with the ash and the ndongu. She rubbed the yellow paste over the wound and grunted her satisfaction. "This wound will heal quickly, but it is good to rest here until morning before going on your journey. *Ignore a wound and invite death.* You and your children are welcome."

"I am grateful," Ma'muriuki said.

"We are glad for you to be with us. We have a question, if the one who is called Ma'muriuki is able to answer us."

"You may ask," Ma'muriuki said.

"We do not see a son called Muriuki among your children. Is your firstborn still among the living?"

Ma'muriuki knew the question was coming, but she still struggled with how to answer it. "My son began this journey with me," she said. She felt her voice tremble a little and tried to regain control. "Ngai has chosen for him to remain among my clan, but I pray that he will be returned to me soon. The world has changed for the Gikuyu people. But I cannot say more, because *the troubles of home are not to be shouted in the field.*"

"*One who guards their tongue is worthy of praise,* my friend. The world has truly changed for the Gikuyu, for *today kills yesterday,*" the woman agreed.

The wives scurried about preparing a meal, scolding Ma'muriuki to sit back down each time she tried to help. They reminded her of the wife she had chosen for her surrogate husband. The women clearly enjoyed serving a guest, and they were not about to let Ma'muriuki ruin their satisfaction. The Gikuyu were fond of saying, *There is always a blessing on the house when one takes good care of strangers.*

"Our new friend is traveling to the land beyond the Mountain of Boys," said the woman who first met the young mother. "I know of a woman in our clan who is going to trade with the Maasai. I think we should talk with her."

"I do not think the medicine man will bless the traders if a woman with children is among them," the first wife said. "But we should ask our husband for counsel and see if he agrees that we should ask for such a blessing. We have goods to send with the traders, so we could take our friend with us that far, as it will still be on her way. But the choice is hers to make first."

Ma'muriuki did not have to think long before answering. "If the traders are along the path that I must take, then I would be foolish to refuse. But I do not think that the medicine man will bless a trip if a mother with children joins the traders. However, I know the Maasai language, and perhaps I could help the traders."

"I see two holes in your ears. I understand," the older woman said. The other women nodded. The first wife then called one of her children to her and gave her some peeled sugar cane. "Take this to our husband in his house so he knows we want to speak to him." The child nodded and ran off.

The afternoon shadows were beginning to lengthen when the husband came to join his wives in the conversation. He sat on a hand-carved, three-legged stool and listened as the women explained what they knew of their guest and her intention to travel with her children into Maasai land. They explained their proposal to take her to the trader women who were leaving in a few days, to see if they would be willing to let her accompany them.

"The world of Ngai is forever changing," the husband said, "when a woman with children has decided to go back to the Maasai. I do not understand such a world. I can call the medicine man to visit me and offer him a fattened goat in exchange for his counsel, but I have never heard of a woman with young children going with the trading women. I think it is more likely the medicine man will curse the journey if such a woman accompanies the others."

"This is a good woman," the oldest wife said. "She has cursed no man in our hearing, and we hear her give instructions to her children about Ngai throughout the day. We do not know why she must go—that is not for us to ask—but she is a good Gikuyu woman. It is always the right of a Gikuyu woman to go back to her mother and father if there is guile in her home. This woman's mother and father live among the Maasai."

"If it is the voice of my wives that I consult the medicine man, I will listen to my wives. It will cost one of those fattened sheep that live in your houses." He paused and looked at Ma'muriuki. "We are a hard-working household, but our place in the community is not as strong as it once was. Perhaps Ngai will return some of the blessings to us if we do good to the strangers in our house. I will call for the medicine man to give guidance for you, but it would not be wise to have hope before we hear what he says. *One who calls for a diviner must accept any verdict.*"

Ma'muriuki nodded and thanked him and the wives for their kindness.

* * *

It had been seven seasons since the husband's brother had negotiated the price of a piece of land with an N'dorobo man and moved his family to the new site a day's journey away. The council advised him to consult the medicine man before leaving with his wife to begin a new community. The brother did not listen and left without a blessing.

During the journey, his new wife became sick and died a few miserable weeks later. Her clan claimed he had caused her death because he had not sought the blessing of the medicine man. They added that he had not completed the bride-price payments and that, because the woman was dead, the balance was immediately due. They insisted on sixty sheep in compensation for her death and one hundred sheep and goats for the balance of the bride-price. This was much higher than the usual demand, but her clan was much stronger and wealthier than the clan of the two brothers.

A council of elders from both clans met and decided it was the brother's negligence that had caused the death of his wife. His clan would make the death payment in full; the brother would pay the balance of the dowry immediately. It was a burden to the entire clan to come up with the payment for the death, but it was devastating for the two brothers to come up with the balance of the dowry. They became debtors to several of the wealthier clan members.

Then the man soon followed his wife in death, leaving his brother solely responsible for the debts. No one blamed him for any of the tragic events, but they felt quite certain that so much bad fortune must be the result of a curse put on the brothers by an angry ancestor or a bad medicine man from the other clan. The wives pulled together around their husband and eventually paid off the debts, but there was little livestock left. The sacrifice of a single fatted lamb for the medicine man was no small matter, but a small blessing from the event could go a long way toward restoring them to the community. It was a risk worth taking.

***

One of the older uncircumcised sons delivered a message to the medicine man that his father was requesting a visit before he gave his blessing or disapproval for the upcoming trade journey into the Maasai land. The father knew, of course, that the medicine man would bring several elders with him to listen to the request and enjoy the fattened lamb. *One should never seek the advice of a hungry man.* Another son informed the leader of the trade expedition that some of the wives were coming with gifts for the journey ahead and a request for one to accompany them, if the medicine man approved.

The messages caused a stir in the community. Most thought that the request to accompany the journey involved one of the wives, and that the family was hoping they had returned to the good graces of the community enough to be able to go on such a journey without bringing a curse with them. While none of the wives could afford to risk the embarrassment of being told they could not go, this was a good way to find out what the sentiment of the community was toward them.

Ma'muriuki, however, was just happy to be off her foot for a few more days. She kept busy by helping the wives pound grains and then wrap the flour carefully in fresh green banana leaves. These would make nice gifts for the trader women. She also helped prepare the feast for the medicine man. The women sent a message to the butcher to cut the lamb. They were not allowed to cook the meat, as the procedure was carefully guarded by the butcher and his helpers, but the women would prepare the porridge and gruel. They also pounded sugar cane into juice. The husband would prepare beer from the cane juices the day before the feast. Even if the results of the meeting were not what they hoped for, they knew that it was never harmful to fill the belly of the medicine man and the elders who accompany him. Ma'muriuki's two daughters spent the time in the fields with the other young girls, cutting grains and pulling weeds. The wives paid her the compliment that her daughters were good Gikuyu girls. The young mother was very proud of them.

***

When the lamb was cooked, the guests filled their bellies with its meat. The butcher and his helpers ate fried intestines and the portions of the stomach designated for cooks only; the wives and daughters ate the parts no man could eat, such as the liver and kidneys. The head, placed in a large clay pot over the fire, simmered in water and stomach juices throughout the cooking process. The soup was soon served, along with the stomach, which was stuffed with the very best parts of the shoulder and leg and then cut into pieces.

As everyone ate their fill, the medicine man kept his eyes on Ma'muriuki. He seemed to know she was the object of his visit.

At last, the husband stood up and invited the medicine

man and the elders to join him in his house. The men grunted their consent. The husband ordered two of his sons to carry the heavy honey beer pot into the house. The men soon followed, bringing the cow-horn drinking cups that had been provided for them. They sat in the husband's hut on three-legged stools surrounding the beer pot and discussed the issue at hand. Occasionally one of them would reach over the beer pot and refill their cow horn by dipping it into the pot.

"You have asked me to come here to speak of the woman and the children who sit among your wives," the medicine man said.

"Yes," the husband replied, not surprised that a medicine man of his stature would understand these things before being told. "She came to us a few days ago with those three children. She has hurt her foot, and we have cared for her because she is a stranger to us. She has not told us why she is here, but she is going to a place beyond the Mountain of Boys, where she once had a mother among the Maasai."

"Your kindness to a stranger is being watched by Ngai, who is the source of all our blessings." The medicine man slowly sucked down some honey beer. "Our world is changing forever. It was once an unheard-of thing that a woman would go back with her children to the Maasai."

"We know that we can send her on her way," the husband said. "But we also know that you will soon be giving your blessing to the traders who are going near the Mountain of Boys."

The elders immediately objected. Such a woman would bring a curse to the entire journey, and she would certainly be captured and kept by the Maasai. The medicine man waved them to silence and turned to the husband. "Is there more you have to say in this matter?"

"Like all of you," the husband said, "when my wives brought this matter to my attention, I objected and said that such a thing had never been done among the Gikuyu and that a journey to the Maasai with a mother and children would never be agreed upon by the traders or the medicine man.

But my wives are wise, and they advised me that this was not a matter for me to decide, but one for the medicine man and the men who sit before me. If such a journey would be blessed by the medicine man, and I neglected to mention it, then it would be my family who would be cursed for my negligence in deciding on a matter that does not belong to me. We have no objection to the decision of the medicine man, nor do we wish to argue what is right in the matter."

"You are not like that foolish brother of yours," the medicine man said. "He was advised to seek counsel and ignored it. You were advised, and you listened and called for our counsel. Now, I will go see this woman."

With that, the medicine man stood up and motioned for the others to stay seated. He stooped as he stepped out of the hut and then walked straight to Ma'muriuki. He motioned for the wives and children to back away from her as she sat stoically on the grass, staring at distant memories.

"My child, it is time to look into you," he told her as he pulled out a bag filled with white powder from the ashes of the mukuyu tree. He sprinkled the powder over her head and on the ground around her and then took some broken bird bones and threw them on the ground in front of her. He studied the bones for a long time before taking a small snuff bag from his waist and inhaling its contents deeply. His eyes widened and dilated, and a white froth bubbled from his mouth. He chanted and flailed his arms and then stopped and slumped to the ground.

No one said a word. Even the men standing at the door of the husband's hut said nothing. The world seemed to stop and wait for the medicine man to return to them.

When he did speak, it startled everyone. They saw him sitting calmly beside Ma'muriuki. Later, everyone would claim that they did not see him get up, but that he just seemed to appear suddenly next to her. But when he did speak, he talked only to her.

"My child, you are a child of Ngai. He knows your distress and will bless you with a long and good life. One day Ngai

31

will return your son Muriuki to your side. Though your heart will be broken yet again, the day will come when you will see your sons together. You should take comfort in this, because *one who stays in the valley cannot get over the hill.* There are many hills in the road before you. I have not yet heard from Ngai about the trading trip, so I do not yet know if there will be a blessing, but I will seek the face of Ngai on your behalf for your journey."

The old man seemed tired, but he stood and waved for the husband and wives to join him. "Ngai has seen the kindness you have shown a stranger. He has not forgotten this family. It will be good if all of you can come to the mugumo tree when I learn if the journey of the traders will have the blessing of Ngai. I will make mention of your kindness to the people." The old man motioned for the elders to join him. Without another word, they left the hedged compound and disappeared.

OKIJABE

Kiserian woke just before the sun broke free of the mountains. Her thin body shivered in the crisp morning air. It was colder than she was accustomed to experiencing in her savannah lands.

The young Maasai girl had fallen asleep hungry. The evening before, she had disregarded the indecipherable chatter of the Gikuyu women as they cooked their meal. Ignoring the voice of the old woman calling to her in Maasai to join them, and the strange smell of the food they cooked, she sat behind an acacia tree with her back to them. Her eyes stared ahead as she tried to drown out their voices and her doubts.

"The stupid Maasai girl must eat or *her pride will be eaten by the hyena tonight.*" The old Gikuyu leader's voice and presence startled the young girl.

Kiserian pretended not to notice when the woman placed boiled yams on a nearby rock. She thought about spitting in disgust, but the memory of her mother's voice stopped her. Her mouth was too dry to spit, anyway.

The Gikuyu woman stared briefly at the thin form of the little Maasai girl before her and then, without another word, turned and rejoined the others.

Kiserian could not resist long and soon broke off a small piece of yam and put it in her mouth. The hunger in her belly exploded in anticipation, and the two yams disappeared in a feeding frenzy. She heard brief laughter from the Gikuyu and felt a little embarrassed at her lack of control. She was still behind the tree, so they may have laughed at something else. Either way, she was not going to let them catch her looking at them. Despite the contented rumble in her stomach, she felt shame that she had been so easily tricked into eating Gikuyu food.

When she heard the women gathering their loads and putting out the cooking fires, she went to the thorn enclosure she had built the night before and let out the cattle. She glanced at the trail ahead. The night before, they had begun a small ascent up the side of the mountain. For Kiserian, who had only lived on the flat savannah land, the trail seemed too steep for the cattle.

"Stupid Maasai girl, you should listen to my voice. *One is clever who listens to advice.*" The old woman reappeared in front of Kiserian. "Above you on the *okijabe* live the N'dorobo. When we are on their land, we will trade with them as we pass through. But our warriors and their wives will see us from our land and will come down to meet us and bring us back. When the night falls, we will be in the Gikuyu lands. We will not allow a Maasai on our lands, and we will not steal a Maasai girl and force her to become a Gikuyu. We have heard the voice of your mother, and we know the will of your father. You must go back to your Maasai family or give us your voice too."

Kiserian knew of the okijabe and the N'dorobo, though she had not been there before. The N'dorobo were very skilled with knives, and the Maasai forced them to perform the cuttings during the Maasai circumcision rites. Kiserian had listened to her older brother talk about his journey with his fellow initiates to the okijabe to find an N'dorobo man for their circumcisions. When they caught the man they sought, they forced him to come back with them to the moran manyatta to perform their circumcision rites. After all, actually performing a circumcision was beneath a Maasai. Beyond their usefulness in this rite, the Maasai considered the N'dorobo to be a useless people who tracked bees for honey and hunted wild animals. Enkai, the great god of the Maasai, had given goats, sheep, and cattle for food, but all wild animals belonged only to Enkai. Because the N'dorobo hunted wild animals for food, they were despised.

Okijabe meant "cold winds." She remembered how cold it had been the night before. Her brothers said that the land of the N'dorobo, squeezed between the Maasai and Gikuyu lands on a plateau halfway up the mountain, was always cold. It was not a place for civilized people.

The cattle did not mind the climb up the side of the mountain as much as the Maasai girl who led them. She found herself breathing hard and felt the sweat running down her back with each step; she had never before climbed up anything higher than the roof of her enkaji and had little concept of the physical stress of ascending a mountain.

When she reached the first plateau above the valley, Kiserian stopped. Her world of expansive savannah grasslands spotted with acacia trees had ended. Before her stood a massive gnarl of unfamiliar trees. She did not think there could be so many trees on earth. Each tree seemed to grow on top of each other and cast dark shadows even in the morning sun. The trail went straight into the trees, and this terrified her. In her world, to stay away from harm such as the lion, one must look far ahead for danger and avoid places where an ambush was possible. Each step into the woods ahead was a step into potential danger.

The old woman came once again and stood beside her. "This is no place for a Maasai girl. I remember when I stood before these woods for the first time, when I too was a young girl."

"The Maasai morani speak of an N'dorobo man in the okijabe who is called Kihereko. My brother met him here when he was seeking the one who does the cutting." Kiserian was a little startled by her own voice.

"You are right, my child. We know this man, too. When the Gikuyu and the Maasai meet to establish peace, they send messages through this N'dorobo man. It is in his fields we will trade with the N'dorobo today. He is useful to both peoples. If you choose to go on with us, you and the cattle should follow the two of us who will lead the way. Behind you and the cattle, the remaining women will follow. We know the forests. You will be safe from what lingers behind the trees."

The old Gikuyu stepped ahead, along with another woman. Both bent slightly under the weight of the load on their backs, the leather straps holding the bundles of merchandise wrapped securely around their foreheads. Despite their burden, the two women chatted with each other as they stepped casually into the forests. Kiserian followed close behind, whistling to the cattle, who snorted back. They too were not used to thick woods.

As they walked the meandering path through the forest, Kiserian occasionally caught a glimpse of the next steep climb looming closer with every step. They crossed a large ravine, the Gikuyu women stepping easily down one side of the gulch and up the other without breaking their stride or pausing to catch their breath in their conversation. Kiserian watched the old women's well-defined calf muscles bulging as they climbed. She wondered at their strength at such an age and if her mother could have kept up with them. Several times she had to touch the ground to steady herself, and she heard the cows complaining behind her as they descended into the ravine. By the time Kiserian and the cows made it safely to the other side, her chest was heaving. Even in the cool day, she felt the sweat on her face and back.

At last, the path came into a clearing. At the far corner sat some strangely dressed people. The old woman turned off the path and walked toward the waiting men and women. As they approached, Kiserian realized that these were the traders. She had never seen a man involved in trading. Both men and women were simply dressed in unscraped skins dyed in faded red and tied hanging over their shoulders. A couple of the men had spears, but most carried bows.

The old woman stopped and waited for Kiserian to catch up with her.

"The cattle can remain here with other items that we have purchased from the Maasai. You can either remain with the cattle or, if you wish, join us as we barter with these N'dorobo. You should know that our warriors will soon meet us here to escort us to our lands." The older woman stared at the girl for a moment and then added, "You should speak to us soon or return to your Maasai home."

Kiserian circled the cattle and made her decision by sitting next to them. Two other women remained behind with her, watching the bartered goods. The girl looked around at the trees that surrounded the fields. A few acacia were sprinkled among them, dwarfed by the others. Up until that day, the acacia was the largest tree in her world. She noticed strange pieces of wood lodged in the branches of several of the trees. They had strange shapes, like very large gourds, but she had never seen gourds that size and could not understand why they had been put there. While she cupped her eyes trying to determine what the objects were, she heard the two women talking. She glanced at them and saw them pointing to her and to the objects in the trees, but she could not understand their language. One of them walked over to her and picked up her herding stick. Kiserian started to grab the stick back and then caught herself. The woman pointed to the herd and gestured that she would take care of the cattle, and then she pointed to the objects in the trees and waved at her to go look at them.

The girl's curiosity was strong, so she walked cautiously toward the objects on the wooded edges. As she approached, she heard a strange sound, like a distant roar of migrating wildebeests. She was startled as first one bee and then another flew past her head and swooped low to the ground. When she stood just a few yards from the base of the tree, she saw a steady stream of bees flying low and then swooping up to the strange gourd above. The bees' bright yellow legs were heavy with pollen. Kiserian had seen bees swarming as they built their honey castles on the branches of the acacia trees in the savannah, but she had never seen ones able to lift large gourds into the trees. It was as strange a sight as the little girl had ever seen.

She walked back to the cows, turning frequently to look again at the gourds. Then she changed direction and walked over to the old woman, who was bartering with an N'dorobo man, and sat down quietly beside her. The woman glanced at her and smiled briefly while she bargained with the man, who carried only a bow. They were arguing over the value of a knife—she refused to sell the tool if the man did not also buy a spear. The man protested that he could not use a spear in the woods. The woman insisted that the spear could be used to barter with the Maasai when they came to find the circumciser. This did not make any sense to the man. When the Maasai came, he told her, they did not bargain, they just took what they wanted. Kiserian agreed this was true, but she did not say anything. Soon enough, he relented and traded some gourds of honey for the knife and the spear.

The man left, grumbling. The old woman turned to Kiserian. "That man wanted the knife so much, I could have sold two spears with it instead of just one."

Kiserian giggled and then caught herself. She pointed to the trees. "I do not understand those gourds in the trees or why the bees fly to them."

"Ah, my child. The N'dorobo have followed the bees into the woods for as long as their memory exists, but we have shown them how to put those wooden gourds in the trees. The bees use the gourds to make their honey, and so the N'dorobo do not have to hunt for them in the woods. Our craftsmen make those gourds with their hands. We have traded them in exchange for much land and honey."

"So the Gikuyu sell the spears to the Maasai and the knives to the N'dorobo? Is there anything that the Gikuyu do not make for others?"

The woman laughed. "My child, the Maasai make their own spears, too, but ours are better, and they would prefer to buy ours than make their own."

Kiserian thought about this for a while. It had never occurred to her that the Maasai might need the Gikuyu more than the Gikuyu needed the Maasai.

"I do not know how to be a Gikuyu girl."

The old woman shooed away an approaching N'dorobo customer and faced Kiserian. "My child, I made a promise to the Maasai woman that I would love you as my own daughter. That is my promise to you, too, when you decide. I will teach you as I have taught the children who came from my own womb. *Growing old and living are the same,* and I am an old woman. My children have children. I know the ways of the Gikuyu. You do not need to know how to be a Gikuyu girl. You only need to choose. I cannot choose for you. My name is Njoki, but because I am a respected grandmother, I am called Shushu." She waved the next N'dorobo over to see her wares.

"Shushu, why do the N'dorobo speak the Maasai language?"

"Most of the N'dorobo on the okijabe were once Maasai, my child. Some were Gikuyu before they were sent away, but most were Maasai."

As the bartering went on, Kiserian noticed that the other N'dorobo showed great deference to a man who was dressed differently from the others. He wore a headband with the black plumage of an ostrich, and the shuka around him was tied with a broad leather belt made from the skin of a leopard. When at last he approached Shushu Njoki and Kiserian, the old woman did not make any effort to show him the same regard. Kiserian started to stand up, but the woman put her hand on the young girl's leg to tell her to stay seated.

"My child, this man is the great Kihereko whom you asked about. Kihereko, here is my child."

Kiserian greeted the man.

"So, your child speaks Maasai too." He made the observation to indicate that he understood who she was.

"This shushu is my mother," Kiserian stated matter-of-factly. The old woman nodded but did not look at her new daughter.

"Will your husband join your warriors in visiting us today?"

The old woman removed a long rope that had been wrapped around her neck. "I untied the last knot in this rope when the sun came up today. My husband has also untied the same knot in the rope at my home. He will join us here. It is our custom that the negotiations begin at the place of the father, but they cannot be completed until they are done before the council of our elders."

"We will follow all the instructions given us. My daughter is willing to be married to your Gikuyu son."

"It is good to hear that you have spoken with your daughter, but we do not force people to become Gikuyu. We must hear from this daughter of yours, and she must agree after she has met our son. But we will not negotiate with the daughter or for her father's land unless they are Gikuyu."

"It will be as you say." He seemed satisfied with the conversation and stood up, briefly touching his chest in deference. The woman acknowledged his gesture but did not return it.

She turned, looked at Kiserian, and smiled. "It is a good decision that my daughter has made."

"Will you have a son for me, too?"

"I will, if you agree, but if you do not agree, there are many young Gikuyu men who may choose you."

"How can I not agree if you are my mother?"

"I am your mother, but you do not belong to me. You belong to Ngai, who is the maker of all things. Now I must do what a mother does to her child when it is time."

Kiserian saw the long, white acacia thorn in her shushu's hand only a moment before the old woman grabbed her ear and pierced the thorn through her upper lobe. The girl shouted in surprise and pain.

"Now, my child, do not touch that thorn. When it is time, I will replace it with a stick until it heals. When this season comes again, I will make another hole in the other ear, and then the next season will be the time for your cutting."

It took several moments before Kiserian could distance herself enough from the pain to speak. She was determined to give no more indication of the pain she was enduring.

"I see that Shushu has three holes in each ear. Will her daughter also have six holes?"

"It is not necessary, my child. The Gikuyu daughters begin when they are younger, and when they have six holes, they know it is time for their cutting. But we show honor to the Maasai mother who raised you, so it is not necessary for you to have six holes in your ears."

"Was your first mother a Maasai, too, and did you become a Gikuyu before the time of the ear piercing?"

"No, my child, I was required to have only three thorns before the cutting. However, I did not want to show the Gikuyu that I was once a Maasai, so I asked my mother to put more holes in my ears. But I want you to know there is no shame that your first mother was a Maasai. I no longer remember the face of my first mother, and sometimes I wish I had not shamed her by hiding my story with my ears. I bring great blessing to my husband and clan because I was once the daughter of the Maasai, and my husband, who is now your father, praises me in the council because I am of great benefit to him and to our clan. If you ask before the cutting, I will put all the thorns of the Gikuyu into your ears, but this choice is not mine; it is yours."

"Shushu, will you give all you have traded to your husband when we cross into the Gikuyu lands?"

The old woman laughed. "My daughter did not talk to me, and I longed to hear her voice. Now I wonder if I will ever stop hearing her questions. But I am pleased; there is much for you to learn. It is true that the land and the animals that

Ngai has given to the Gikuyu are to be cared for by the husbands, and the homes and people that Ngai has blessed us with are to be cared for by the wives. However, when a wife trades goods with the Maasai, they are hers to keep, even the cattle. I will keep a few of the cattle for myself for milk or an upcoming feast. Most of the cattle I will give to my husband. He too will keep some of the best cattle to strengthen our herd. The rest will be divided between members of our clan, council elders, and the medicine man who blessed our trip. This will strengthen our place in our clan, which is a blessing to my husband and his family. So while the animals are mine to keep, I choose to bless my husband with my success. It is also true that a wife does not have the time to raise animals and cultivate the shamba and teach her children."

"I do not understand the word shamba," Kiserian said.

"Ah, my child, that is because the Maasai people only raise animals for eating. The Gikuyu prepare land in a place called a shamba, where they place seeds and plants and grow the vegetables, arrowroot, bananas, and other foods that Ngai has given us."

"I do not like the food that does not come from animals," Kiserian said. "It hurts my stomach, but it stops my hunger."

The old woman chuckled. "It will not be long before the food you do not like now becomes the food you want to eat the most. The food of the Gikuyu is not like the Maasai, but the Gikuyu do not go to bed hungry."

"So does my new Gikuyu father own many cattle? If he does, he could be a great Maasai too."

"The Gikuyu do not own their livestock; rather, Ngai blesses them by allowing husbands to take care of the animals. All things are owned by Ngai. I do not own you, but you are a child of Ngai. I will care for you because Ngai has blessed me with the gift of a daughter."

"Will I come back to the Maasai lands with you when you return to sell goods?"

The old woman smiled again. "The Maasai do not harm a Gikuyu who is a grandmother, but they would try to steal you back like they will these cows if you go with me while you are still young. When you have a grown child of your own, you will be welcomed back with me to the Maasai lands. You will not be harmed then, and you would be a great blessing to your husband."

"Will you tell me the story of Ngai?"

"Many times, my child, but for now I want to sell these knives and spears to these N'dorobo for honey and skins, so that my journey home is laden with what I have purchased rather than what I could not sell."

With that, Kiserian sat quietly, watching her new mother barter for goods.

MUGUMO TREE

"Mama, why do we meet under the mugumo tree?"

Wangari's constant barrage of questions reminded Ma'muriuki of how many questions she had asked her Gikuyu mother. She was determined never to grow tired of explaining the world to her children.

"Because Ngai has instructed us to offer a sacrifice at the mugumo tree whenever the counsel of the one who gave us this earth is sought. Today the medicine man will find out if there is a blessing for the traders' journey to the Maasai. He will also seek the counsel of Ngai about whether we can accompany them."

"Do you think Ngai will bless our journey too, Mama?"

"We will be blessed, my child, because we love Ngai and we do no evil or curse others."

They were sitting on a grassy knoll alongside the clearing, watching the gathering crowd of people who came to hear the words that Ngai would speak to the medicine man. Soon an old Gikuyu woman came and sat next to them. Ma'muriuki greeted the lady in Gikuyu, but the woman answered in Maasai.

"It is rumored that you wish to accompany me to the Maasai lands with your children," she said.

"I wish only to listen to the voice of Ngai," Ma'muriuki replied. "If there is a blessing for me, I will go with you, but I would not be one to bring a curse to you or your journey."

"I do not think such a request has ever been made before," the woman said.

Ma'muriuki did not detect any opposition to the idea in her voice.

"Did your first mother live near the Mountain of Boys?"

"She lived beyond it, near the Angry Mountain. But I was young and do not know where she is now, or if there are any from my manyatta who still live."

"There are not many manyattas near the Angry Mountain these days; the world has changed too much. But if I go ahead without you, I will ask the people I trade with if they know of your clan and send word to you."

"You are kind to me." Ma'muriuki had always understood how important it was for a child of Ngai to treat strangers with kindness, but it had been years since she was on the receiving end. "Tell me, was your first mother also from among the Maasai?"

"She was," the older woman said. "I have made many trips since I became a shushu, but most of my clan has died, and the few who remain joined other clans. But tell me, my friend, who was the shushu who received you from the Maasai?"

"My first Gikuyu mother was called Shushu Njoki. She adopted me from my Maasai mother when I was young. She now rests beneath the mugumo tree with her husband. She was a great woman among my clan."

"I remember her well," the old woman said. "I have seen her at the great trading markets between the Maasai and the Gikuyu. *While Maasai and Gikuyu men fight, their women barter.*" The old woman glanced back at the crowd and stood up. "I see it is time for me to join the ceremony. My husband is the one there holding the goat. I hope only peace for you."

"And I you," Ma'muriuki said. She noticed an elderly man holding a goat by a rope standing next to some women at the back of the crowd.

"Mama! What were those strange words between you and that woman?" Wangari asked.

"Ah, my child, that is the Maasai language."

"Maasai! Mama, you speak the language of lazy thieves?"

Ma'muriuki smiled to herself as the memory of her first encounter with the Gikuyu crossed her mind. "Child, compared to the Gikuyu they may be lazy, but they are fierce warriors, and while at times we fight with them when they steal our cattle, they have helped us keep our borders safe from the Swahili, who want to take our children and sell them to others. We are good for the Maasai, and they are good for us."

The crowd started singing songs about Ngai, about how he gave the lands to a man named Gikuyu and took him on top of the Shining Mountain to show him the land between four mountains that he had given him. Gikuyu then journeyed to a place among the mukuyu and mugumo trees, where he found his wife, Mumbai, waiting for him, and they made their home among the trees. "Ngai now invites his people to seek him under the mugumo tree," they sang.

"But, Mama, I do not understand why Ngai chose the mugumo and the mukuyu tree."

"My child, it will take a lifetime to understand the reasons, but here are two, one for each tree: Ngai is like the white, shining sand on the side of the Shining Mountain. Ngai is pure and white. We do not cut down the mukuyu tree, but when a branch falls to the ground, our medicine men burn it in the fire, and the ash is as white as the white sand on the mountain. No other tree burns such white ash. The medicine man mixes the white ash with the fat of a sacrificed sheep to paint his face when he approaches Ngai with a request. So, my child, the heart of the mukuyu tree is pure like the heart of Ngai."

"What about the mugumo tree, Mama?"

"Patience, child," Ma'muriuki said. "The mugumo tree gives fruit like the mukuyu tree, but it is very different. Often its seed will grow in the branches of another tree. As it grows, it sends its roots to the ground. It wraps its roots around the roots of the other tree and slowly takes the nourishment from the earth until it becomes mightier than the tree it grows on. Finally, the time will come when the other tree disappears inside the roots and bark and branches of the mugumo tree until one can no longer find the first tree."

"Mama, what does that mean to Ngai?"

"Child, Ngai put the Gikuyu on these lands, which were occupied by others such as the N'dorobo and the Gumba. The Gikuyu have never been to war with these peoples, and we have never taken the lands that Ngai gave us from them. Instead, like the mugumo tree, the roots of our people have grown throughout the lands, and these other people have become more dependent on us than on their own traditions. They sold us their lands as we grew, and most of them became one with us, until there were no Gumba left on earth, and there are very few N'dorobo.

"Ngai has made us to be like the mugumo tree. Even now, the spirits of our ancestors rest under the roots of these trees. Ngai also has promised to listen to our requests when we make sacrifice and prayer under these trees."

"Mama…"

"Hush now, child. *Two waterfalls cannot hear each other.* Listen and watch, and then you can ask your questions."

The mugumo tree was an ancient specimen. The base looked like giant cords twisted together that scattered out in every direction on the ground. The shade of the leaf-laden branches was so thick, for much of the day the sun never shone directly on the trunk.

The medicine man sat with nine elders along the edge of the shade cast by the mugumo tree. He wore a large headdress made from the black-and-white fur of the colobus monkey. Plumes of black-and-white feathers from the male ostrich dangled from the monkey skin. A line extended down from the top of his head, dividing his nose, mouth, and chest, down to his colobus monkey loincloth. On one side, he was bare; on the other, he was colored white from the mixture of white ash and sheep fat. The white reflected brilliantly as the man rocked between the sunlight and the shade. To the side of the tree, butchers were preparing goat meat for the celebration that they hoped would follow.

The singing stopped, and the crowd parted as the women planning the bartering trip to the Maasai lands walked toward the tree, led by the husband of the woman who had talked to Ma'muriuki a few minutes before. The women sat down in a tight group as the husband led the goat to within a few feet of the medicine man and the elders.

The medicine man stood up. "It is not right to disturb Ngai for trivial matters, for those things we must settle among ourselves. It is not right to ask foolish questions. But you have come to ask a favor of Ngai, so speak your mind, but do not speak of trivial matters."

"I will speak the matter plainly," the old man holding the sacrificial goat said, "and then I will let others judge if the matter is too trivial. My wife has often gone among the Maasai to barter our goods. These trades have been of great benefit to my family and our clan." He swept his hand across the people sitting nearby, and his gesture was met with shouts of affirmation from the crowd.

The medicine man raised his hand to silence them.

"I cannot give my consent to my wife," the man continued, "unless I know that this trip is approved by Ngai and that there will be no bad omens or curses on the way. It is of great benefit to us if she goes, but the cost of a bad spirit being released is too great to go without a blessing. I have nothing else to say on this matter, but I have brought my best goat for sacrifice."

"Are there any other matters that I should understand first?" the medicine man asked.

"I have heard that there is another matter with a woman and her children who are strangers to us," the man holding the goat said. "I do not know about that matter but am told that it has already come to your attention. My wife has told me that this mother is a good woman and she would be useful on the journey, if such a thing could be blessed by Ngai."

"I know of this matter," the medicine man said. "Speak no more about it." He motioned for the man to bring him the goat.

The man did as he was instructed and then backed up a few steps and sat down. The elders came forward quickly and held the goat while the medicine man pulled a sharp knife from a sheath at his side and plunged it into the goat's neck. The animal struggled wildly and then stopped as his blood poured into a large gourd on the ground.

When he was satisfied that there was enough blood, the medicine man ordered the elders to hold the dead goat upright while he counted four ribs from the belly and plunged the knife into the back of the animal, severing it in half. He cut down both sides, and then the elders folded the back open. The stomach and intestines poured onto the ground. At his word, the men took the goat aside and began to skin and butcher it for the burnt offering to Ngai.

The medicine man separated the stomach from the rest of the viscera and poured some of its contents into the gourd of blood. He set the remainder of the stomach portions aside for the elders to prepare and laid a length of the intestines in a circle around the trader wife's husband. The rest of the intestines he circled around the women, until he had laid out all of the entrails. He then took a bag of crushed bird bones and feathers and threw them on the ground, first in front of the husband and then in front of the women. Finally, he took some white ash from the mukuyu tree and sprinkled it over the man and the women.

The crowd fell into a hushed silence as they watched the medicine man carefully study the patterns of the scattered bones and feathers. He stood up and walked under the shade of the mugumo tree, where he took out a snuff bag, inhaled deeply, and quickly collapsed to the ground.

The elders called for the butchers to bring coals from their cooking fires. They came and quickly lit a fire next to the tree. The flames roared to life as they caught the abundant kindling and dry wood. The sacrificial portions of the goat were thrown on the flames, which quickly consumed them, sending a dark cloud of smoke through the leaves high above and into the blue skies.

When the medicine man suddenly appeared sitting next to the other elders, he spoke in a loud and clear voice. "Ngai is pleased that the women sitting in front of me have sought a blessing for their trip. They will be kept safe on their journey, and if they follow all the ways Ngai has given the Gikuyu, then the journey will be successful for them and for our clan."

The medicine man turned to the husband in front of him. "You have sought counsel from Ngai. Your home will be kept safe, and there will be no bad omens on your house while these women are on their journey."

He then turned his attention to the husband and wives who had taken Ma'muriuki into their home. "It is good that the people of my clan listen to my voice. That man is not like his brother, who brought trouble to our clan. He is a wise man who seeks counsel and does not neglect to listen to the voice of others. Ngai is pleased with him because he has paid his debts and his brother's debts. This is a man of blessing and peace; he does not bring bad omens to our clan."

Ma'muriuki watched the faces of the husband and his wives as they took in this news. She could see the flood of relief on their faces as they were welcomed again into the good graces of their community.

Finally, the medicine man turned his attention to Ma'muriuki and her children. "Ngai has said that there will be no blessing for the journey if Ma'muriuki becomes part of the traders' group. It is not right for a young mother and her children to be part of the trading. If she is with the trading women in the Maasai lands, then the women will be attacked by the Maasai, who will steal the mother and her children for themselves." He paused to let the effect of his words sink in.

There was a silent hush as most eyes turned to Ma'muriuki.

"However, Ngai is not finished with his words on this matter. He has shown me that this is a good Gikuyu woman who is faithful to Ngai and to her family. Her suffering will not be forever, and her words to Ngai have been heard. Ngai has permitted the mother and her children to accompany the traders until they reach the okijabe and she can see the Mountain of Boys. When she sees the mountain, she must go a separate way, but she will know that Ngai will not forget her. She and her children will be protected among the Maasai."

The crowds milled around the husband and the trader women, congratulating them, as Ma'muriuki sat alone on the hill with her children. Makena moved close to her mother and leaned quietly into her. Wangari turned to ask a question but saw that Ma'muriuki was close to tears. She sat down on the other side of her mother and held her.

"Did the daughter of Ngai hear my words?" The voice startled them, and they turned to see the medicine man sitting next to them.

Ma'muriuki struggled to regain her composure. "I heard."

"Remember the saying: *The oldest son is the same as the father.* Your son, Muriuki, will regain his inheritance, and you and your children will see the day of his honor. *Wealth and poverty are never strangers.* As for the one from whom you run, remember: *The case of a fool is taken up by Ngai while the fool sleeps.*"

Ma'muriuki nodded and smiled at her children. When she looked back to the medicine man, he was gone.

51

CROSSING RIVERS

Early in the early morning, Kiserian sat across the river from her Gikuyu home. Her mother had given her detailed instructions for this day, and the young girl felt a small shudder of excitement and apprehension.

One season had come and gone since she left the Maasai and began her new life among the Gikuyu. Even the elders at the council told her that she was learning to speak Gikuyu very well. Her mother, however, spoke often to her in Maasai. The old woman told her daughter that she must not forget her childhood language, because it would be of great benefit for her and her family when she was old enough to go on trading trips.

The sun had not been up long, and the air was still cold. She sat alone wrapped in a red-dyed goatskin. Her face and arms were smeared with red ochre mixed with sheep fat. She wore multiple strands of Maasai beads around her neck.

Next to Kiserian was a makeshift Maasai hut that she had made by herself. Her new family sat on the other side of the river and quietly waited. The hut was simply constructed with sticks crudely pushed into the ground and a flat roof plastered with a mixture of cow manure and mud.

While she built the hut, her extended family made a makeshift Gikuyu hut of their own on the other side of the river. In the Maasai world, the construction of the hut was the work of the women alone. In the Gikuyu world, it was always a community effort.

The silence was interrupted by the medicine man running out of the trees on the Gikuyu side, screaming and waving his arms as he forded the river and charged toward Kiserian. She jumped up and ran into her hut.

"The Maasai girl dies today and a Gikuyu girl is born from the womb of the shushu, Njoki," the medicine man shouted. His face was streaked with white ash, and he was wrapped in the skin of a leopard. His headdress, made from the white and black hide of the colobus monkey, bobbed as he danced around the hut, calling an end to any evil spirits or curses that may have followed the girl when she came from the Maasai.

He ordered Kiserian to come out of the hut and leave any memory of the Maasai behind her. She emerged from the hut completely naked, having left everything inside. The medicine man danced around her, commanding any remaining spirits to depart from her. He circled around to the back of the hut and emerged from the other side carrying a firebrand in each hand. He placed the brands into the walls of the hut, and soon the entire structure was engulfed in flames.

He shouted to Kiserian to go to the river and wash the Maasai from her flesh. She stepped into the cold water and shuddered.

***

It was not the cold alone that caused her to shiver. For a Maasai, a river was considered taboo and too risky to cross. The fish in the river were seen as revolting, the hippo and crocodile too dangerous. Even the water itself was deemed unclean and not fit for humans to drink. Only the cattle were allowed to drink briefly at the water's edge and then were quickly moved away before the river's hidden dangers could attack. Kiserian's shushu had shown her how the Gikuyu made bridges from fallen trees as a way to cross most of the rivers in the Gikuyu lands. But they rarely used the bridges, except during the heavy rains. They had few hippos in their lands and fewer crocodiles, and they did not fear the water. The bridges were hidden on the sides of trails, so that any raiding Maasai warriors would be slowed down during their all-too-frequent raids on Gikuyu livestock. Kiserian made certain she knew where all the bridges were around her home, as the idea of fording a river still terrified her.

***

But this time she stepped into the river and fought to ignore her terror. When the water was up to her knees, she sat down and washed the ochre off her body. Then she stood, shivering uncontrollably as she turned and showed herself to the medicine man.

"Now the Maasai girl must die forever," he commanded. "It is time for the Maasai girl to drown herself in the river."

Kiserian turned again and stepped her way slowly to the deepest part of the river. The medicine man followed close behind her, chanting curses against the Maasai intruder. When she reached the middle, the water swirled just above her waist and she dropped beneath the surface. She grabbed a large rock to hold herself down and to keep from being swept downriver. She stayed under as long as she could—until the sheer panic of being underwater for the first time sent her head bursting out of the river amid wheezing gasps of air. A few moments of terror-stricken panic accompanied uncontrollable gagging and coughing as she tried to expel the water she had taken in.

The crowd cheered at the spectacle. Kiserian regained enough composure to take a step toward them and slipped on a rock. The medicine man grabbed her arm to steady her.

"Careful, my child. We did not want the Maasai girl, but we refuse to lose the Gikuyu girl."

She smiled her thanks as she muffled the urge to begin coughing again and then focused on the sounds of her new extended family shouting encouragements to her. Remembering her shushu's instruction, she stopped just short of stepping out of the water, her body still shivering uncontrollably.

"Who among you is a mother about to give birth to this child?" The medicine man took Kiserian's arm again as he asked the question.

"I am the mother expecting this child," Shushu Njoki said. "If it is a boy, I will praise Ngai for bringing the owner of the lands to our home; if it is a girl, I will praise Ngai for bringing the giver of life to us." She stepped to the front of the crowd.

"Where then is the mother's womb so this one can be born?" The medicine man grabbed and shook Kiserian's arm once more.

Two men emerged from the back of the crowd carrying a banana leaf that was taller than Kiserian and held it in front of her by the edge of the water. The medicine man took a knife and split the leaf from top to bottom. The men held the two halves of the leaf together. The medicine man then stepped between Kiserian and the leaf, pushed a gourd through the split, and poured water on the ground on the other side. "See, the water has come from the womb. The child is ready to be born." He stepped around the leaf to the opposite side of Kiserian. "Who is here to help this mother with this child?"

"We are here." Two women emerged holding two colorfully dyed Gikuyu blankets in their arms. They stood in front of the banana leaf on the opposite side of Kiserian and laid the blankets on the ground. They reached into the opening of the leaf and motioned for Kiserian to put her head through it.

"The child is alive," one of them shouted.

"Do you know if it is a boy or a girl yet?" the medicine man asked.

"We do not know yet, but when we see, we will shout for the whole community to hear." The women gently pulled Kiserian the rest of the way through the leaf. They gave four shrill ululations as they wrapped the skins around the girl's shivering body.

"Who has heard the shout of the women?" the medicine man asked.

"We have, and it is the blessing of a girl. Ngai has sent a giver of life to our clan," the crowd shouted in unison.

Shushu Njoki put her arm around Kiserian and led her to the Gikuyu hut. "Leave me and my child in peace for eight days," the old woman said, "so that I can welcome her to this world as a mother should."

Kiserian and her shushu spent the rest of the day sitting in the shade of their hut, visiting with the steady stream of well-wishers. The walls of the quickly built hut were made of loosely woven sticks, making it easy for the two inside to see and be seen by those on the outside.

Soon the smells of roasting goat meat, honey beer, and the sweet scent of yams filled the air. The feast was put on by the shushu's husband who, according to custom, was expected to feed his kinfolk upon the arrival of a new child.

Through the crude walls of the hut, Shushu Njoki and her new daughter could see the men sitting around the big honey beer pot, drinking with their cow horn cups. The shushu's son, Waitimu, seemed to be doing most of the work, keeping people happy with gourds filled with food or bitter gruel to drink. The shushu noticed Kiserian watching Waitimu serving the guests, just as she had observed her watching him as he worked in the shamba.

As the feasting began to slow just before nightfall, Shushu Njoki turned to Kiserian. "Now, my child, the season has come when I must do what a mother must do." The girl saw the long white thorn in her shushu's hand. The old woman grabbed her ear and pushed the thorn through the lobe. "When this season comes again, you will be ready for your cutting."

Kiserian had been expecting the second thorn for several weeks and had prepared herself for the event. Other than a brief grimace, she gave no indication of the pain.

The onlookers nodded in approval of her response. "This one," they said, "is a true Gikuyu."

THE GIKUYU TRAIL

"Mama, I don't understand the marks on the path," Wangari said. "They look like the tracks of two heavy snakes traveling together. But even a heavy snake could not make a mark so deep in the ground."

Ma'muriuki had been trying to make sense of the long parallel grooves herself. "I do not know, my child. I too have never seen such marks. When it is time to stop and rest, we will ask the trading women."

They had been following the women along the ancient trading route for several days. Despite the heavy loads on their backs, the women kept a steady pace across the tops of ridges and down into ravines. They refused to let Ma'muriuki share their burdens. Her duty was to her children and theirs to their trading. Ma'muriuki preferred to follow behind so she and her children would not interrupt their pace. Sometimes she would stop and breastfeed Maathai, or the children would play briefly, chasing butterflies or poking sticks at a line of army ants, and then they would hurry to catch up with the traders. The women seemed to enjoy the company of Ma'muriuki and her children.

The owners of the shambas along the trail had constructed booths on the path, the makeshift roofs shading fresh fruit and vegetables left out for travelers. What had begun as a goodwill gesture toward strangers had become a matter of competition between the wealthier landowners. Each constructed a more elaborate booth and put out larger quantities of food in an effort to outdo the others. The women knew which booths had the best food and stopped and ate whenever they came to one.

In front of just such a booth, the leader of the women called a halt. The traders quickly set their loads on the side of the trail, picked through the food, and ate. Ma'muriuki sat down and fed Maathai as Wangari and Makena followed the women. Soon the girls returned with sweet bananas and boiled yams.

"My children, you have brought too much food to eat at one time."

"Mama, there is so much food there, we can take some with us too."

"No, my child, one may eat from the kindness of others, but one who takes more than they eat is a thief. *A bird flies from the shamba only with what it has swallowed.* We do not have any goats to pay the fine for such theft." Ma'muriuki set aside some bananas and arrowroots. "Now each of you take a little to eat for yourself and then return the rest quickly before we are accused of theft."

The girls gathered up the extra bananas and tubers and took them back to the booth. They returned with the old woman in charge of the trading party. "I see you train your children well in the ways of the Gikuyu," she said. "We live in days when everything is changing, and our children are forgetting our ways."

"It is a task that has no end," Ma'muriuki said. "It is not just children who are forgetting. A Gikuyu woman is no longer the owner of her home and her husband is no longer the owner of the land."

"This is true," the old woman said. "There are too many *ahoi* among the Gikuyu, and they no longer act according to our ways. We will suffer if we keep forgetting the ways of

Ngai." They sat in silence for a few moments, the older woman waiting to see if Ma'muriuki wanted to say more, and Ma'muriuki trying to find a way to change the subject.

"My children and I have a question for you. We have seen these strange tracks on the path. I do not remember seeing these markings, and I cannot explain to my children what kind of animal makes such tracks."

"These markings are made by the Butterfly People," the old woman said. She picked up a stick and drew a square shape in the dirt path. "They use very large cattle to pull boxes made of wood and skins. The boxes are carried by feet shaped like the moon." She drew circles beneath the square shape. "It is the feet shaped like the moon that touch the ground as the boxes move, and they leave these marks in the ground."

"The Butterfly People have come this far into our lands?"

"Sometimes they travel on this trail but do not stop. We do not know what they are doing or where they are going."

"You have seen these Butterfly People?"

"I have seen them from a distance. Some of our clanspeople have seen their spears shoot lightning at trees, piercing holes right through them. Even animals at great distances fall to their death from the lightning spears. They have very powerful magic. Some call them 'Red People.' Their faces turn red in the sun. They hide from it. Their women wear the clothing of butterflies, and they sit on the boxes. I do not know if their feet ever touch the ground. They are unclean people. They kill and eat the meat of animals that Ngai has protected."

"How long will they live among us?"

"Mugu Kibiru said that they will stay until the great mugumo tree that sits with his clan dies, but most say that the strangers will soon get tired and go back to their own lands. But they are very strong, and Mugu Kibiru warned us that we cannot go to war with them until we have learned their magic for ourselves. This is why we do not fight them."

Ma'muriuki hoped she would not meet these strangers.

"Not many in my clan have seen them," she said. "Yet my clan is changing because of them. They have powerful magic."

The old woman put her hand gently on Ma'muriuki's shoulder. *"This is the business of Ngai."*

"It is the business of Ngai," Ma'muriuki agreed.

"Our medicine man warned us not to talk to the Butterfly People on this journey, because we do not yet understand them. They are somewhere on this path ahead of us. They are a very noisy people, so it is easy to know when they are coming. If they come, we will hide in the trees or in the shambas until they pass by. We do not want them to put a strange curse on us that our medicine man cannot break."

The old woman stood up and went to her load of trading goods. She sat on the ground and placed the wide leather strap that bound the load together on her forehead. She rocked back and forth several times and then stood up. The load weighed more than the old woman, but she gave no indication of stress under its burden. Soon all the old women were moving down the trail under their heavy loads. Ma'muriuki sat with her children, watching them go.

"Mama, who are the Butterfly People that the medicine man spoke about?" Wangari asked.

"Child, Mugu Kibiru is a great medicine man among the Gikuyu people. When I was a child, not much older than you, he had a great vision while sacrificing a goat to Ngai under the great mugumo tree. He told us that the Butterfly People will come up with the Swahili from the great waters. They will bring magic spears that speak with lightning and that no Gikuyu warrior could defeat. He said they will bring a great snake that will come across the Gikuyu lands, and upon that snake will ride a giant monster that breathes fire and runs like a centipede. The monster will swallow great numbers of people in one place and vomit them out in another."

"Are those markings on the path the markings of the giant snake of the Butterfly People, Mama?"

"I do not know, my child," Ma'muriuki said. "But listen to

the voice of your mother. I do not know these people, but the great medicine man said that we must learn their ways before we can be strong enough to defeat them. There will come a time when you will need to learn the ways of the Butterfly People, and then you must teach those ways to your children until we can defeat the Butterfly People and send them back to their home."

"I do not like the Butterfly People, Mama," Makena said.

"I fear them too, my child. But Ngai does good things for the Gikuyu. I do not know if the Butterfly People will be good or bad for us. Perhaps Ngai has better things for us after they are gone."

"Mama, do these people fly like butterflies?" Makena asked.

"No, I do not think so, but I think their clothing is made from the bright and colorful wings of many butterflies."

"Mama, butterfly wings break too easily for clothing," Makena said. "Do they have very strong butterflies in the home of the Butterfly People?"

"Perhaps when they see how easily our butterfly wings break, they will go home." Wangari smiled bravely at her little sister.

Ma'muriuki stood up. "We should stay closer to the women until the tracks of the Butterfly People are gone." They hurried after the traders, who had disappeared around a bend in the path.

The traders carefully eased their way down into a ravine, Ma'muriuki and her children not far behind. Then the older women all stopped abruptly across the shallow stream. Ma'muriuki could hear the alarm in their murmurs and instinctively grabbed her girls and pulled them to the side of the path, ready to run into the forests if needed. The women turned around and quickly made their way back to Ma'muriuki.

"What is up ahead that causes the traders to turn around so quickly?"

"We do not know what it is," the older woman said. "It

appears to be a dead buffalo, but the head is gone."

"It is best that we climb up in the trees and wait to see if others are around this dead animal," Ma'muriuki said. The leader nodded.

"Mama," Wangari said, "if the buffalo is dead, why do we need to climb trees?"

"I will answer you, child," Ma'muriuki said, "after you are safely in the trees."

The older women quickly dropped their loads and scaled the surrounding trees with low hanging branches. Two of them waited until Ma'muriuki was up a tree and then handed her children to her one at a time before climbing to safety themselves.

"Children, listen to my instructions about the buffalo." Both Wangari and Makena turned around on their branches to face their mother, who held a sleeping Maathai in her arms. "You have not seen the buffalo because you have lived in the safety of the shamba. But the buffalo is to be respected, because it is very fierce and strong. The buffalo work together like the Gikuyu people. When one is attacked among them, the others will try to find revenge. We do not wait here for the dead one; we wait to see if others are returning to have their revenge."

Soon all of the women were safely in the trees and out of reach of any vengeful buffalo. They began to chatter.

"How does a buffalo lose its head?"

"It is a very big one. What animal can kill a buffalo and eat only its head?"

"Perhaps N'dorobo have come up here, but are they so foolish as to run away with only the head and leave the best meat behind?"

"Is it possible that this was the work of the Butterfly People?"

"What would the Butterfly People need from the head of a buffalo?"

"Is the head of the buffalo where their great magic comes from? Perhaps they have run out of buffalo where they are from and have come to take ours."

Ma'muriuki watched the sun work its way through the trees. There were very few hours left before darkness. She did not want to spend another night in the woods. "Listen to me," she said. "We have waited here and our talk has not attracted the attention of the buffalo. I think they are gone. I ask my friends to watch my children so that I can go look around this buffalo and see if it is safe for us to travel. If we do not leave soon, we will spend the night here and the buffalo will not be our only concern. I knew the ways of the buffalo when I was young. I will be safe."

None of the women wanted to venture near the dead animal, but it was not right for the mother of young children to do what they were afraid to do. No one wanted to stay the night in those woods, open to the eyes of predators and the curses of angry ancestors. "My daughter, you are a brave one," the leader said. "But I too knew the ways of the buffalo when I was very young. There is no choice but for the two of us to go together. One of us can watch the bushes while the other watches the tracks."

Ma'muriuki did not wait for any other conversation. She dropped out of her tree and handed Maathai to the other women to take care of while she was gone.

"When we signal, I hope that you will bring my children to me," she said. The women agreed. Ma'muriuki turned to the old woman now standing beside her. "I was too young to remember what kind of sticks my mother used," she said.

"These are the ones," the old woman said as she broke off two green sticks and handed one to Ma'muriuki. Both women quickly broke the sticks into little pieces and placed the sticks between each toe. They lifted their hands over their heads and spoke loudly.

"What is my mother saying?" Wangari asked.

"Your mother is speaking in the Maasai language, child. Your mother speaks the words that give them safety from strong animals."

Both women lowered their hands and walked toward the

dead animal. They did not hurry—nothing in their movements indicated any concern for what they were doing. The women in the trees peered down at them anxiously, commenting on their progress.

"They have crossed the water."

"They are walking around the dead animal now, looking at the road. They are looking for signs of other buffalo."

"One is kneeling by the buffalo while the other is looking at the bushes."

"They are waving at us."

"Come children, let's go to your mother. We should not stay in this place anymore."

Ma'muriuki waited for her children. She scooped Maathai into her arms and wrapped him with the long cloth on her back with help from Wangari. She reached for Makena's hand and led her children behind the other women and past the dead buffalo. Each woman paused briefly to stare in sickened silence at the dark red spot where the head had been. No one spoke while they climbed up the ravine to the other side. It was not until they reached the first shamba that the leader broke the silence, hailing the houses behind the compound. A voice called out from the other side of the hedged fence, "Do I hear the voices of strangers?"

"We would be strangers, except your mother was my sister when we were still young," the old woman called back. A delighted shriek and a clamber of voices came from behind the hedge as the gated barrier was removed. A woman about Ma'muriuki's age appeared, embraced the old woman, and urged everyone to come in. She wedged the barrier behind them.

There was a collective sigh of relief. The women chattered to each other and to the women emerging from the various houses, explaining what they had experienced, trying to understand it themselves. The confusion eventually broke into laughter as meals were prepared and conversations settled onto more comfortable subjects.

The traders learned that the Butterfly People had passed

by earlier that same day, but they did not seem to notice the compound. The Gikuyu living closer to the Maasai land were adept at hiding their compounds from passing strangers. The women in the compound said that they had heard some thunder in the ravine before the Butterfly People appeared, which was strange because there were no clouds in the sky at the time.

At the evening fire, the men came and sat with the women. A very old man was led to a log by a young boy. They all wanted to hear the trader women's story about the dead buffalo.

After listening to their report, the old man stood up. Everyone knew he had something to say and fell silent. He leaned on his staff while the young boy held his other arm. "The Gikuyu people have a story from the ancestors that tells how Ngai expects the Gikuyu to respect all animals.

"The story begins in the time when the Gikuyu women still ruled over the men. In those days, Ngai divided the animals of the earth between men and women. The women were given all of the animals to eat, except for the cattle, sheep, and goats, which were reserved for the men. In those days, the women only had sharp sticks and wooden knives with which to slaughter their animals for food. The animals suffered greatly. This displeased Ngai so much that all the animals given to women were taken from them, and Ngai caused them to become wild and untamable. They were under Ngai's protection, and the Gikuyu were no longer allowed to eat them.

"When the men saw what Ngai had done to the women, they became afraid, and they went to the mountain of Ngai and offered sacrifices and prayers, asking for guidance, so that they would not also lose the animals given to them.

"Ngai was very pleased that the men had sought advice. Ngai told the men to follow the great river until they reached the place of black sand. They were instructed to take the sand and heat it. They then were to pour the iron that came out of the sand into molds and make knives so they could slaughter their animals without cruelty. The men rejoiced and thanked Ngai. Ngai instructed the men that though all the remaining animals that could be eaten belonged to them, they must be kind to the women and share portions of the meat with them.

"This is why, even to this day, as a sign that they understand Ngai's instruction, men share the choice portions of the animals that Ngai has given them with their women. And other portions such as the kidneys and liver are to be eaten by women only.

"Since this time, it is understood by all Gikuyu that all wild animals, which once belonged to women, are protected by Ngai. No Gikuyu person who has killed a wild animal can remain Gikuyu. Such a person is banished from among our people and sent to join the worthless N'dorobo. But even the N'dorobo kill only what they need in order to eat."

The old man concluded his story and sat down to make his point. "I hope that I may live among the ancestors before I see the Butterfly People face to face. It is hard to imagine what evil curses come with people who do not respect enough what they have stolen from Ngai to take the meat as well. Such people cannot be good to know."

They all sat silently, thinking about what the old man had said. The world was turning upside down, and their own prophets had told them that they would be unable to stop it. Never before had the Gikuyu people allowed strangers to come to their lands. Never before had they felt so utterly defeated, and there had not yet been a fight.

"Mama," Wangari said. "I do not want to see the Butterfly People, either."

"What is a child doing among the trader people?" the old man asked. "Did the trader women get the blessing of the medicine man before going on this trip?"

"We have a blessing," the old woman said. "It was the medicine man who told us to take this child and her mother with us. He told us that no curse would come to us because of this woman and her children. And they will not travel with us into the Maasai lands."

"That is good," the old man said. He was clearly relieved. "It is not safe for a young mother with children to be among the Maasai."

Wangari started to speak, but Ma'muriuki placed her hand over her daughter's mouth. She smiled with as much confidence as she could muster. Wangari looked at her mother and said nothing.

SHAMBA

Shushu Njoki and Kiserian worked together on the banana crops. Kiserian cut off the ripe clusters from mature stalks and placed supporting stakes under immature ones. The shushu cut down the mature banana plants that Kiserian harvested to allow the new plants emerging from the old roots room to grow. It was one of Kiserian's favorite tasks in the shamba because it gave her and her shushu plenty of time to talk. Both had removed their shukas and wore only a loose sheepskin around their waist.

Since Shushu Njoki, her husband, and Kiserian were the only people left in the household, the shamba was small. Each day, when they finished the daily tasks in their small field, the shushu and Kiserian would climb over the wooden stile that separated their shamba from the land of the shushu's widowed son, Waitimu. They cultivated and planted behind him as he broke new ground.

Working behind Waitimu was Kiserian's favorite task in the shamba. It seemed that since her formal adoption by her Gikuyu clan, working in Waitimu's shamba had become increasingly important to her.

"Shushu, my cutting will be in one season. I will then be eligible for marriage?" Kiserian asked.

"Yes, my daughter, but there is no reason for you to hurry into marriage. After the cutting, many young warriors will dance with you at the festivals. When your heart becomes mended with another, that is the time to think of marriage."

"Shushu, a circumcised woman cannot marry someone from her own clan?"

"This is true; it is a vile and disgusting thing to marry someone from one's own clan. This is why the young circumcised men and women go to dances all over Gikuyu land, so that they can find good mates from other clans. But you should learn which clans are good—our clan does not allow marriages with some clans because they carry bad omens or curses."

"Shushu, does this mean that I cannot marry someone who belongs to your clan because I am now your daughter in the eyes of the Gikuyu?"

"It is true that you are now considered to be born from my flesh, but the Gikuyu council does not forget that your first mother was a Maasai, as was mine. They will allow you to marry even someone from my clan. There will be no prohibition of this kind for you."

"Will the Gikuyu find a surgeon among the N'dorobo to do the cutting, like the Maasai?"

"No, my child, we have our own surgeons who do the cutting," her shushu said. "You have much to learn, but the first thing we must do is look for an honorable elder and his wife to become your Gikuyu mentors. These mentors will guide you through the cutting and will become your living guides as long as they walk on this earth, and they will be your ancestor guides when the time comes for them to dwell beneath the mugumo tree."

"Shushu, why do I need a guide? Are you not my mother and guide now?"

"Yes, my child, I am your mother. But these mentors become representatives to you on behalf of all Gikuyu. It is good to have the voices of many to guide you in the journey ahead, and your mentors will be the most important of those voices. They will instruct you in your duties as a woman when my time to instruct you as a mother has passed.

"You will stay in their house for eight days to mourn the end of your childhood. Then they will bring you to the elders for approval on the day before the cutting. They will stand with you when you declare your oath to our people. The wife will hold you during the cutting so you do not move. It is they who will help you heal after you become a woman and they who will give you the secret instructions on the Gikuyu ways known only to those who have been cut. At that time, you will no longer be my daughter in the same way you are now, for you will belong to Ngai alone. I will always be your mother, and your second loyalty will always be to me and to your family."

"Will my first loyalty be to my Gikuyu clan?"

"No, my child. Do you remember nothing? The first loyalty of every Gikuyu is to Ngai. It is Ngai who gave us this world and told us to cultivate the ground to honor our creator. The second loyalty is always to the family. It is through the womb of your mother that Ngai has chosen to bring you into this world. Because Ngai has blessed your family by giving you to us, you must return the blessing to your family as your first offering of thanksgiving to Ngai. Your third loyalty is to the Gikuyu people."

The two reached the end of the banana plants. The old woman beckoned for her daughter to follow her. Kiserian picked up a small cluster of ripened bananas and followed her shushu. She knew it was time to work in Waitimu's shamba.

***

Shushu Njoki had three grown daughters. All three lived with their husbands on distant ridges that belonged to their husbands' clans. She also had two sons. The oldest son married an N'dorobo woman whose father had negotiated a land-purchasing agreement through the shushu. The Gikuyu did not purchase lands unless all parties were Gikuyu, so the N'dorobo family was adopted into the Gikuyu people, and the marriage became part of the land-purchase agreement.

The son left with his new wife to begin a new homestead on the purchased land, near the okijabe.

The second son was Waitimu. He was the youngest of the five siblings and his compound was just behind the shushu's. Waitimu had been married for a very short time when his wife died during her labor, along with their unborn child. It was rumored that the cause of the woman's death had been a curse on her from an angry ancestor. After her death, Shushu Njoki's clan placed a ban on any future marriages from the dead wife's clan. After all, the Gikuyu had stronger and better clans from which to pick a mate; there was no reason to risk a curse from an angry ancestor.

***

The stile that gave access to Waitimu's compound stood at the corner of three shambas: Shushu Njoki's, Waitimu's, and a third cultivated by tenants. The shushu climbed over into Waitimu's shamba first. As Kiserian climbed to the top of the fence, she was able to see into the tenant lands. Two women and a young girl worked in a far corner of the field, almost out of hearing distance. Almost was good enough for a Gikuyu.

"*Mwemwega*," Kiserian's voice boomed.

All three tenants stood up and waved at her. "*Demwega*." Their voices carried back to Kiserian. She returned their wave and climbed down to join her shushu.

"Shushu, why do the Gikuyu call these people ahoi?"

"Ahoi are ones who are born among the Gikuyu but have lost their land or are too poor to buy land. We call them ahoi because there is no honor among the Gikuyu if one does not have land to cultivate a shamba for their family.

"Sometimes one becomes an ahoi and it is not their fault. However, if one who is ahoi does not show that they are working hard to regain land, they are not considered to be true Gikuyu."

"Why do you allow such people to work on your lands?"

"There is also no honor in a clan that has ahoi living among them—it can be a matter of shame if other clans learn that ours has too many ahoi. It is the responsibility of the wealthy to allow ahoi to regain their honor by loaning them land to prove that they are not too lazy or foolish to be among the Gikuyu."

"Shushu, what happens to a person who does not work hard to gain land and wealth?"

"Such a person would be sent out of the clan, and most would become N'dorobo. But if an ahoi shows that they work hard and are accumulating property and wealth, then they will regain respect in the community. This is good for them, and it is good for the clan."

"Shushu, I think the Maasai do not give a person such a chance if they have lost their cattle. Is this why there are more N'dorobo who are from the Maasai than from the Gikuyu?"

"This is true, my child," the shushu said. "It is the wish of every Gikuyu that all who are among us own land, so that we honor Ngai together. We do not want to lose true Gikuyu who have lost their land due to misfortune or angry ancestors. It is also of great benefit to my husband and myself when we help a good ahoi to regain their place among the Gikuyu. The bond between them and us cannot easily be broken."

***

Between her many bartering trips, the dowry payments for their three daughters, and careful management of their resources, Shushu Njoki and her husband managed to accumulate considerable wealth and influence in the clan. They purchased tracts of land with some of their cattle and sheep, but they still maintained a respectable herd.

Because they had no uncircumcised boys left in their household, they leased small herds of their livestock to poorer clan members. In exchange for the care of the animals, they allowed the less fortunate to keep for themselves every other calf or lamb born. They also allowed the few Gikuyu families in their clan without land of their own to become tenant farmers on the large, unused portions of their lands.

***

The two walked between the planted rows toward Waitimu. His back glistened as he drove the heavy digging pole into the earth, breaking new ground on the far edge of his field.

Most of a Gikuyu's day was spent in the shamba. Men and boys took out trees and bushes in their never-ending attempts to increase the available areas for cultivation. Once an area was cleared, the men then pounded into the ground with a long sharp pole and turned the soil. The women and girls worked behind the men, beating the turned soil to break it down, removing any remaining weeds, and sowing the seeds or tubers for the new crops.

Division of labor was not strictly applied, however. Women would aid in the land clearing if the men were behind, and the men would refine the soil and sow if the women were behind. It was common for a widower like Waitimu to do all the work by himself. It would never be proper for him to ask his mother and Kiserian for help, but it was not shameful that he accepted it.

Waitimu's task at hand was to get millet planted before the short rainy season began. As the two women came up behind him, he paused briefly and smiled at them before he turned again to his task. He was naked except for a skirt of braided long grass and banana leaves that hung loosely from his waist. His back and arms rippled as he stabbed the ground with his digging stick and turned the soil.

Kiserian quietly came up beside Waitimu and placed the bananas she had carried with her next to him. She paused and looked at him. He smiled again.

"So the Maasai traitor has come to poison me with food?" he asked.

"Yes, and when I poison you, I will steal all your cattle and bring them back to my Maasai father where they belong." She faced him, pushing forward her budding breasts.

Waitimu laughed, shook his head at her, and returned to his digging stick.

The young girl enjoyed working on Waitimu's land; she enjoyed his friendly banter during their short rests. She returned to the side of her shushu and began speaking in Maasai.

"Why do the Gikuyu sometimes call me a Maasai traitor?"

"Ah, my child, even my husband calls me a traitor. But they say it with respect, and every Gikuyu man who marries a Maasai traitor is thankful for his good fortune. I have given my husband wealth from my trading work with the Maasai. Most Gikuyu women can only give their husbands wealth by giving them children and by sharing their labor in the shamba."

She handed the young girl a pounding stick that was about as long as Kiserian's arm. It was a thick piece of hardwood with one side worn flat from use. Both women began to pound the turned soil behind Waitimu, progressing forward little by little as the soil was loosened enough for planting. After every ten steps of progress they stopped pounding long enough to poke shallow, evenly spaced divots about the length of a human foot along the freshly cultivated soil. They then sprinkled millet seeds in each hole and covered it with dirt. One handful of seed was enough for ten paces of soil.

As Kiserian worked, she frequently glanced up at Waitimu. Several times she caught him watching her as he dug into the ground. It became a game each day for her to see how many times she could catch him watching her.

Even the shushu could see the little game the two played and how they teased each other throughout the day.

"Shushu, tell me, what will happen after my cutting?"

"After you are healed, you will be eligible for marriage. You will go to many dances with your age mates throughout the Gikuyu clans. You will dance with warriors looking for wives."

"Will it only be warriors who will be at the dances, Shushu?"

"It is a great event and everyone from the nearby clans join together for the celebrations, but the dances are meant for warriors to meet the women."

"Must a circumcised woman be chosen only by a warrior?"

"No, my child. If no warrior chooses a woman during the time for marrying, there will be other ways for her to marry. The Gikuyu have a saying: *Even an ugly Gikuyu woman will find a husband.* Do you understand this saying?"

"I have heard of that saying, Shushu. It means that if a woman is not chosen by any warrior, she will become the second or third wife of a man with many cattle. This way, every woman will have an opportunity to give life to the community."

"You have understood the saying well, my child. It is usually the wife who chooses another wife for her husband, when there is too much work in the shamba for her."

"Shushu, how does an eligible woman know if a warrior is making an offer to marry her?"

"My child, it is a long process, but it begins when a warrior who is dancing with you puts his hand on your shoulder. When he does this, it means that he is interested in you."

"What does the woman do if she is also interested in him?"

"If she is interested, she will step on his feet. They will dance together with her feet on his."

"Is there any shame if she does not step on his feet, Shushu?"

"There is no shame, my daughter; there is only shame on him if he insists when she is not willing."

"If she steps on his feet, does that mean they will ask for permission to marry?"

"My child, I think you already know these things. The two will have many days during the dances to get to know each other and decide if it is a right thing. But even then, it takes some time before they will inform the parents of their decision."

"I know these things, but is there shame if a woman does not step on the feet of *any* warrior?"

"There is no shame, my child, but it is the duty of a Gikuyu woman to bring life to the community. One who does not look for a husband could bring great shame to herself and her clan."

The shushu stopped working, stood up, and glanced in the direction of the afternoon sun. Her husband, who was on the council of elders, was having a meeting at his house the next day, and she needed to make some juice from sugar cane so that he could prepare the beer for the meeting. He would mix the juice with fermented millet and the ground-up bark of the *muratina* plant. With these three ingredients on hand, beer could be prepared the day before it would be consumed.

"Come child," she said, dropping her pounding stick on the ground. "We must prepare for my husband's meeting."

Kiserian dropped her stick and followed the old woman out of the shamba. She took one last look over her shoulder and caught Waitimu leaning on his digging stick. He was watching her. She smiled and waved shyly. He pretended to ignore her and resumed turning the soil.

The two walked through a small stand of sugar cane at the edge of the shamba and broke off the tallest stalks at the roots. Once they each had an armful, they carried their bundles to the pounding trough. The trough was a long log with a hollowed channel on one side. They placed two canes at a time in the channel and took turns pounding the fibrous stalks with long, heavy wooden poles, until the last of the cane juice flowed into a gourd at the lower end of the log. With each swing of the pounding poles they narrowly missed each other's hands, and they depended on keeping a steady tempo to avoid injury. Occasionally, they would pause and the shushu would clean out the pulped remains while Kiserian picked up fresh canes and placed them in the log. Then their rhythmic pounding would resume.

Kiserian switched the conversation back into Gikuyu. Her shushu noticed she was asking more questions than usual that day. She guessed what was behind her inquiry but chose to let the young girl get to the real question at her own pace.

"Shushu, how does a woman find a way to step on the feet of someone who is no longer a warrior at the dances? Do any others dance with the women, too?"

"My child, the dances go on for several seasons. When there are women who do not find warriors after a few seasons, other men who are looking for wives will join the dances. Usually this happens when a man's wife thinks she needs more help in the shamba. She comes to the dances and finds a young woman for her husband. Then the wife sends her husband to the dance to find the woman she has chosen for him."

"Shushu, will Waitimu ever be at the dances?"

The old woman stopped, put her hands on her hips, and stared at her daughter. But Kiserian knew her shushu well enough to know the old woman was not really angry.

"My child, it is no longer my time to give my son instructions, nor will I shame him by doing so. If he dances at the festivals, it will be his choice."

"Shushu, I know that these things belong to Ngai, but I do not want to put my feet on those of a warrior if I can someday put my feet on those of Waitimu."

"My daughter, soon you will have your cutting, and I will no longer be one who can give you instructions as one does a child. When you ask for advice, I will give it, but I will not give you instructions. I will not shame you or my son on this matter."

"I know this, Shushu. But my heart thinks this should be. I remember when you first adopted me from my Maasai mother; you told me it may be that I would one day become the wife of your son. I have not forgotten your words. I think it would be a good thing."

"My heart would rejoice, my daughter. But this is in the hands of Ngai."

Kiserian nodded. She knew her shushu would find a clever way to communicate the matter to Waitimu without shaming him.

The old woman had heard no rumors indicating that

Waitimu was ready to look for a new wife; he seemed content to work in his shamba and oversee his livestock. Early each morning he picked up the digging stick and would pound and twist it into the soil for much of the day. The hard work seemed to distract the widower from his troubles.

She knew that it would be a difficult task for Waitimu to find another wife. No one held him directly accountable for his first wife's curse, but parents of eligible women would be very reluctant to give their daughters to him for fear that the curse had come on him as well. Shushu Njoki had new hope for her son when Kiserian came into their lives. It seemed like a good thing was happening.

THE SNAKE HAS COME

As Ma'muriuki walked with her children behind the trading women, she noticed that fewer of the ridgetops were cultivated. Gradually, all evidence of Gikuyu farming disappeared and the trail became surrounded by the thick overgrowth of virgin forests.

"Mama, why are there no shambas here?" Wangari asked.

"My child, we are near the end of the Gikuyu lands. People do not cultivate these lands in order to make it harder for the Maasai invaders to find us. Any Gikuyu shambas are hidden by the woods far from this trail. Soon we will be in the lands of the N'dorobo, and the world will change for us."

"The N'dorobo hunt animals that Ngai has protected, like the Butterfly People do," Wangari stated. "Do the N'dorobo only eat the heads of the animals too?"

"No, my child. The N'dorobo hunt the animals, but they apologize to the spirits of those animals, because they must feed their families. I do not know the way of the Butterfly People, but I do not think they have concern for the spirits of animals."

A few hours before the sun went down, Wangari pointed to the women ahead. "Mama, why are the women unloading their burdens so soon in the day?"

"Children, look beyond the women. Do you see any trees?"

"There are no trees, Mama. What does that mean?"

"That is where the land of the Gikuyu ends," Ma'muriuki said. "The whole world falls below our lands. First, it falls to the okijabe of the N'dorobo, and then it falls to the lands of the Maasai. We will spend our last night with our friends here where they have stopped."

The old woman stood to meet Ma'muriuki and her children as they approached. She pointed to a large, flat rock at the fork in the trail, perched at the edge of a great valley. "I know it has been a long time since your eyes have looked upon the Maasai lands. If you take your children to that rock, you can show them the place of your birth. We will prepare the evening meal when you are ready to return."

Ma'muriuki nodded and motioned for her children to follow her. They had no difficulty climbing on top of the rock. "My children, take my hand but do not be afraid—we will sit near the other end of this rock, and I will show you what tomorrow will bring for us."

With the baby firmly on her back, she took the hands of her girls and walked them to the edge. The girls gasped and took a slight step backwards. "Do not fear, my children, we will sit. I will not bring harm to you."

The world dropped several thousand feet to the valley floor, the forests plunging down the side between rock cliffs and waterfalls. Dark purple mountains pierced through the clouds far across the valley. In the breaks between the clouds, the sun shed light on the vast grasslands below.

"I think, my children, that this must be what the eagle sees when it is above us."

They did not hear her as they tried to understand what they were seeing. The girls slowly relaxed their grips on their mother.

"Can my children see that little mountain that sits between us and the tall ones?"

"I see it, Mama," Wangari said. "It looks like a cow resting on the ground."

Ma'muriuki laughed. "My child, your eyes are full of imagination. The Maasai people call it the Mountain of Boys. I remember that as a child I was told if a boy ran around it seven times, he would turn into a girl. No one could tell me what would happen if a girl ran around it seven times."

"Have you climbed that mountain, Mama?"

"Oh no, child, such a thing could not happen. But look beyond that little mountain to the big one, called *Ol Doinyo Nyokie*. There are times when Enkai of the Maasai speaks from that mountain. Beyond that mountain was the manyatta of my father, where I was born."

"Are we going to that place, Mama?"

"We will go there, my child. I do not know where the relatives of my Maasai mother and father are living, but perhaps someone there can tell us where to find them."

"Mama, do you remember the faces of your mother and father when you were a Maasai?" Wangari asked.

"I sometimes remember the face of my mother, but I do not remember that of my father. I remember that my mother called him Naengop."

"Mama, how will you find the family of your father and mother?"

"I do not know, my child, but I will give the names I remember to others among the Maasai, and perhaps they can tell me where my clan now lives."

The children sat staring at their future far below. Soon the old Gikuyu leader came to tell them the evening meal was ready. She then sat next to the children on the rock.

"Mama, what are those big rocks among the trees in the place of the N'dorobo?"

Ma'muriuki looked carefully in the direction where Wangari pointed. She had been gazing beyond them to the Maasai land and had not noticed the strange formations. They looked to be big rocks with a shiny top that glistened in the filtered sunrays. There were four or five of them, and one seemed to have a hazy smoke next to it. "I do not know what that is, my child; my eyes do not remember these types of rocks."

"Those are caves that belong to the Butterfly People," the old woman said. "They bring rocks from the rivers and build caves above the ground. We do not know why they live in caves. No one has seen what they do inside of them."

"I do not understand," Ma'muriuki said. "I thought the Butterfly People were strangers. Why would they build caves on the N'dorobo lands? Do they not have homes where they came from?"

"No one understands the Butterfly People," the old woman said, "but the world is changing everywhere they go. Do you remember the prophecy of the great snake and the beast that rides on it?"

"I remember the prophecy," Ma'muriuki said. "I think those markings we saw on the trail behind us must be those of the great snake."

"Oh no, my child, the snake is below you when you enter the N'dorobo lands. It has cut a deep wound in the earth and you will know that it is the snake when you see it. You must find a way to get over it, because it has no beginning or end. Some Gikuyu have walked many days near the snake to find the head so that they can kill it, but they went far into lands beyond our neighbors before they lost heart and returned."

"How does one cross over it?"

"The elders think the snake may have bad omens, so they urge the Gikuyu not to touch it, in case one contaminates the rest of the Gikuyu people. We place branches from trees on it and walk across so that our feet do not touch it. But from time to time, the great beast that breathes fire and vomits people only to swallow them again comes riding atop the snake. This is a dangerous time for a Gikuyu. You must hide from this great beast. We do not know if it sees you, if it will swallow you as it goes past. You must keep your children quiet and hidden if it comes."

"I will not know if the beast is coming."

"It shakes the earth and makes a terrible roar. You will

hear it approaching before you see it. That is when you must hide. Do not wait."

Ma'muriuki sat in silence, trying to make sense of the old woman's words. "We can see the Mountain of Boys from here," she said. "In the morning, we will go on another path from those of the traders. I remember the instructions of the medicine man."

"Yes—it is with sadness that we will leave you," the old woman said. "You have been a good companion to us. Watching your children play along the way has made our loads lighter." She pointed along the ridge to the right. "Our path goes along this ridge and then down this mountain on the other side of the Butterfly People's caves." She pointed to the left of the rocks. "Your path goes down below this rock. You must be careful, because it is not far from the caves, and it would be better if they do not see you." The old woman paused for a moment. "Do you know why the Gikuyu traders no longer travel near the Mountain of Boys?"

"No, I do not know the reason you now go another way," Ma'muriuki said.

"There are some Gikuyu from another clan who joined with the Butterfly People," the old woman said. "It was during the time when the great snake first came through our world."

"I had heard that some of our Gikuyu people from other clans have joined with them," Ma'muriuki said.

"It was not long ago when those Gikuyu were traveling with the Swahili and the Butterfly People that the Maasai went to war with them and killed them by the Mountain of Boys."

"I do not understand," Ma'muriuki said. "When has a Gikuyu ever traveled with the Swahili? Why would our people travel on Maasai land if they were not women traders?"

"No one understands the Butterfly People," the old woman said. "No one understands why a Gikuyu would do what a Butterfly Person tells them to do, even if it brings them death. No one understands what power makes a Gikuyu travel with a Swahili."

"Did our people go to war with the Maasai for killing so many of the Gikuyu?" Ma'muriuki asked.

"No," the old woman said. "We did not go to war with the Maasai because we understood why they fought. We do not understand what those from our clans did.

"Did the Butterfly People go to war with the Maasai?"

"No. I am told that even the Butterfly People understood what the Maasai did. Because the Butterfly People did not fight the Maasai, many from among the Maasai have joined with the Butterfly People."

"I do not understand the Butterfly People," Ma'muriuki said.

"I too do not understand," the woman replied. But understand this, the Mountain of Boys is a place of death, and many angry ancestors may dwell there. I know you must travel near the mountain to find your people, but you must be careful and not test the ancestors when you are near that place."

"We are grateful to the traders for taking us this far," Ma'muriuki said. "My children and I will not forget your words or your kindness. My clan lived beyond the Mountain of Spirits, which is beyond the Mountain of Boys. We must go there and see if we can find anyone who remembers our clan or knows where they now live."

"That is good," the old woman said. "We will go to the big trees past the Mountain of Anger. We will ask about your clan along the way. If we learn of anything, we will let the Maasai people know that there is a mother and her children looking for her clan near the Mountain of Spirits. It is a difficult path you have chosen, but we can see that Ngai has not left you."

"Even though I have never seen these Butterfly People, they have changed my clan forever," Ma'muriuki said. "I did not choose this path, but I must take it."

"The Gikuyu world is forever changed," the old woman agreed. "I do not know what it is that Ngai has for us, or why we are forbidden to fight the Butterfly People when they come to our lands uninvited."

"Come, children." Ma'muriuki said, "The sun will not be with us much longer, and it will be a cold night. We should find a place near the fire."

***

Ma'muriuki and the children carefully worked their way down the path toward the N'dorobo lands. It was not as steep as it appeared from the top, as they descended along a large staircase of ridges. In the steeper areas, the children crawled down backward.

"Mama, can a cow make it up this path?" Wangari asked.

"Yes, my child. Many do every year. It is easier for them than it is for us. But when you get used to this path as the traders do, you do not hesitate but walk up and down like you would on flat ground."

The ground leveled off near the N'dorobo land. "This is a good place to rest. There will be no more steep paths until we get beyond the N'dorobo," Ma'muriuki said. She sat on a rock surrounded by a small glen and told the girls to stay where she could see them.

It was not long before the girls were chasing each other through the small field, laughing and running after small birds and butterflies. They wandered toward the trees at the edge of the glen while Ma'muriuki watched.

Suddenly, the girls came to a stop, frozen in their tracks, and then turned and hurried back to their mother, their arms flailing as they ran in silent terror. Ma'muriuki scooped up Maathai and met them. "Mama, it is there!" They pointed behind them.

"I do not see it. What is it that you see, children?"

"The snake, Mama! It is the snake," Wangari said breathlessly, fear mixed with tears in her eyes.

Ma'muriuki scooped up her youngest daughter with her free arm. "Follow me, child," she said to Wangari, who walked closely behind her. Ma'muriuki passed the edge of the glen and crouched behind a big tree. The girls huddled quietly next to her.

"My child, did you see any Butterfly People?"

"I do not understand what it was I saw, Mama. It must be the snake, but I did not see anything else. I was too afraid to look."

"That is good, child. We do not want to be seen until the medicine men tell us it is safe to meet a Butterfly Person without being cursed."

"Mama, I want the Butterfly People to go away."

"I want them to go too, my child, but our medicine men say we may have to learn their magic before we can make them leave."

"How long before we can make them go away, Mama? Are they with the Maasai too?"

"I do not know, my child. I hope we will never see them. Now follow me, I must see this snake and decide how to get across it."

"Will it move, Mama?"

"I do not know, child. Now be quiet and follow me. You must listen to my voice."

"I will listen, Mama."

Ma'muriuki worked her way between the trees, staying away from the open field. When she reached the end of the glen, she motioned for Wangari to hide behind a tree. She handed Maathai to her and motioned for Makena to sit next to her sister. "Wait for me here, children. Do not stand up or follow me. I will return to you."

She left the children there and walked along the trees next to the path until she came upon Wangari's discovery. She ducked behind a bush and studied the creatures before her, but she did not understand what she was looking at. The two snakes were smaller than she had imagined, and their skin looked like the iron of a spear. They seemed to be sleeping as they lay on a path built of black wood and gravel. They rested a footstep apart as far as she could see in either direction. A shiver went up her back. Even though they did not move, Ma'muriuki was certain they were alive. She had no choice but to cross over them. She could not turn back. She looked around for a way to cross over the snakes without touching them, but there were no trees near enough to form a bridge. She made a pile of branches heavy with leaves along the edge of the woods, but out of sight of the snakes, and hurried back to her children.

"Follow me quickly," she said to Wangari as she scooped up Maathai and took Makena by the hand. She quickly retraced her steps and placed her children in the bushes, well hidden from the tracks. "Stay here, and I will make the way across the snakes for us. Do not come out or follow me until I call for you."

"Yes, Mama," her children answered.

Ma'muriuki gathered some branches and stepped into the clearing next to the snakes. She glanced in both directions to make certain no one was around. She did not see anyone, but what she did see sent a wave of terror through her. She had not anticipated the sheer power of the snake. It cut its giant footprint right through the sides of the mountain as far as she could see in both directions. She forced herself to return to her task and set branches upon the small ridge of rocks that lay crushed beneath the snakes. The wooden posts between the rocks were as black as the night. She could only guess that the wood had been burnt by the anger of the snake or by the beast that rode above the snakes. She carefully laid some branches between the snakes.

She was laying down the final portion of her bridge when she heard something in the near distance. It sounded like a human voice, but a strange, foreign voice. She knew at once that she had been spotted by the Butterfly People. She looked up and saw forms that were only barely human. They were shouting and running toward her from the other side of the snakes.

Ma'muriuki hesitated only a moment before she turned and ran back into the woods, close to where her children hid. She hoped that if the Butterfly People followed her, they would not see the children. She made her way quietly back to where they huddled in shaken silence with faces clearly relieved to see their mother. Wangari was holding Maathai with her hand over his mouth to keep him quiet. Ma'muriuki took her little son in her arms and dropped down with her daughters. She looked back at the tracks to see if the Butterfly People had followed her.

She could see them clearly, standing above the snakes and looking toward where Ma'muriuki had run into the trees. One of them spoke with the angry voice of a man as he threw off the branches Ma'muriuki had carefully laid on the snakes. He was covered with the skin of a white butterfly and his head was covered with a strange white headdress. The other person, who spoke with a woman's voice, was wearing the skins of many colored butterflies. They flowed down from her shoulders, and it was not possible to see a human form under the many skins. The one with the woman's voice held something in her arms that might have been a baby Butterfly Person. Ma'muriuki thought she could hear the soft sounds of a crying child. It was strange to her that the child was in the Butterfly Woman's arms.

When the man had finished clearing the branches from the snakes, he stood for a moment looking in the direction that Ma'muriuki had run, and then he went and rejoined the woman on the other side of the snakes from Ma'muriuki and her children. away from the snakes. They both stood and looked quietly along the length of the snakes in the same direction to Ma'muriuki's left. They seemed to have forgotten about her.

"My children, there are some Butterfly People out there standing by the snake. I will watch them and tell you when it is safe for us to move. It is important that you stay quiet until they are gone."

"Mama, can I look at the Butterfly People?" Wangari asked.

"It is okay, my child. I know other Gikuyu have looked at them, and there is no known curse from this. But we must be very careful that they do not see us."

Wangari rose from her crouch and then quickly dropped down as the earth began to shake. A deep rumbling sound unlike any earthquake that Ma'muriuki had heard before seemed to be coming toward them.

"Mama, what is that shaking sound?"

"Hush, child. I do not know. We must stay hidden." The rumbling grew louder. The ground seemed ready to rip apart. Ma'muriuki saw the Butterfly Man lift his hands high in the air. Then came a terrible piercing cry that she knew did not belong in the forest.

"Children, this must be the beast that rides on the snakes. We must not let it see us." The mother and her children lay on the ground hidden in the bushes, shaking with fear. Ma'muriuki occasionally lifted her head to be certain that the Butterfly People did not come to her side and point out her location to the beast.

She saw the front of the terrible monster appear and block out the Butterfly People. The beast was screaming loudly as white and gray smoke billowed from the fire in its breath. It moved slower and slower until it stopped. She lay quiet for a time and then lifted her head, as the beast seemed to be resting right in front of her. She could see the legs of the Butterfly People under the belly of the beast. The first time she looked, it was just the legs of the man and the woman. The next time, she saw several more legs of Butterfly People. Then she looked again. All the legs had disappeared.

She waited, her whole body trembling.

The beast screamed again. Smoke billowed from its mouth as it began to move away slowly, then faster. When she looked again, it was gone. She could not see the Butterfly People. Still, she waited.

"Mama, are those the Butterfly People who live in the stone caves we saw from above?" Wangari asked.

"I do not know, my child. One of them was holding a baby. I think it may be that they build the caves for when they have babies. Perhaps when they finish having babies, they will all go back to where they came from."

"Mama, are they gone now?"

"I think the beast and the Butterfly People are gone, my child. I do not know their ways, but I do not think they have the power to see us in the dark. We will wait until night to get across."

Ma'muriuki and her children waited while the sun climbed into the heat of the day and then drifted toward the mountains. As the long shadows accompanied the early evening breeze, she gathered the leafy branches again. In the dusk, she built a new path over the snake, got to the other side with her children, and found a place to hide again for the night.

"Mama, I do not like the Butterfly People," Wangari said. "I want them to go to their homes and leave us alone."

Makena moved close to her sister.

"The day will come, my child, when you may know these Butterfly People. Our prophets have said that they will live among us for a long time. Perhaps even your children's children will know them. One day we will understand them, and then we will not fear them."

"Mama, I wish that our brother Muriuki was here."

"My heart longs for him as well, my child, but this is a matter in the hands of Ngai. Now we must sleep. The journey is not over."

THE DEATH OF CHILDHOOD

Kiserian sat naked on the grass, her body still glistening from the river. She spread her legs wide and put her elbows on her raised knees. Her gentle Gikuyu mentor, Wanjiku, sat behind her and pulled her back slightly against her breasts. The woman wrapped one of her legs and then the other around Kiserian's thin body, placed them between the young girl's knees, and spread her legs further apart, locking her into position so she could hardly move.

"You are a good child, but today you become a good Gikuyu woman. Do not be afraid. This is a time of rejoicing for you."

"I do not fear pain, Shushu Wanjiku," Kiserian said. A cold sweat of adrenaline mingled with the river water on her body. "I have learned the lesson of pain and am ready to become a woman." She glanced back at the old woman and then to the tight gathering of her female Gikuyu relatives pressed up close behind her, watching and waiting, ready to encourage her to be brave when the cutting began.

"That is good, my child. It is a shame if a man shows pain when he is cut, but it is not expected that a woman will show no pain. It is a great honor for her, however, if she is fearless and does not cry out too much. I will place my hands

91

over your eyes before the surgeon begins, as it will calm your fears."

"Today my honor will be the same as the boys sitting under the other mugumo tree. I will not need your hands over my eyes," she replied.

"That is not necessary, my child."

"It is my wish; you will not be disappointed in me."

***

Eight days earlier, Kiserian began her eight days of mourning. It was the time to mourn the end of her childhood and learn her responsibilities as a Gikuyu woman. She spent the days in the home of Shushu Wanjiku, the Gikuyu mentor that her mother had chosen for her. A close friend of Shushu Njoki, Shushu Wanjiku would become her advisor on all the stages of a Gikuyu woman's life for as long as the mentor lived. It was said that the mentor would continue to watch over Kiserian even after the woman departed to live with the ancestors. Kiserian stayed in Shushu Wanjiku's house on what was once the daughter's bed. The bed was empty, since all of Shushu Wanjiku's children had long since been married.

The young girl and her mentor spent most of the time talking together in the house. Once a day, just before nightfall, Kiserian was allowed to go outside the hut and sit in a clearing with the other young initiates, in order to become acquainted with her new age mates. Kiserian stood out because she had only two holes in her ears. The other girls, all with six holes in their ears, knew that she had been adopted from the Maasai. One of the girls, Kijeko, sat next to Kiserian each day. It was clear that Kijeko was the leader of the group, because each girl showed her deference. A bond between Kiserian and Kijeko grew quickly, and soon the girls were showing deference to Kiserian as well.

Kiserian's mentor gave instructions to her about the days ahead and the expectations placed on her once she became a Gikuyu woman. She learned the requirements for taking care of her mother, Shushu Njoki, and for her loyalty to her other age mates and her absolute fidelity to the Gikuyu people.

At first light on the morning of the cutting, Shushu Wanjiku and an assistant shaved all the hair off the young girl's head and body. They covered her face with a white mask made of sheep fat mixed with mukuyu ashes. Finally, they wrapped her in a single shuka made from soft sheepskin.

At the distant sound of four ululations, Kiserian's mentor led her out of the house and to a field where the other young female initiates stood. Five more ululations followed, and a row of young boys came out of their huts and stood in a line separately from the girls. A council of elders sat in a semicircle on three-legged stools, and a white goat lay struggling by the elders' feet, its legs bound tightly together with leather. The mentors of each initiate led their charges in front of the council, and the elders began the Ceremony of Oathing. The young people swore loyalty to Ngai, to their family, to the Gikuyu people. Then one of the elders stabbed the goat in the throat with a knife and turned the blade until the blood from the dying goat began to spurt.

"May you die like this goat if you break your oath to the Gikuyu," the elder declared.

"May it be done to us," the initiates shouted in unison.

Then there was a shout, and the race began. Earlier that morning, an elder had marked a mugumo tree in the forest. Each initiate raced into the woods, looking for the tree. The first ones to find it would become the leaders of their age mates. Kiserian slowed down when she saw the tree to allow Kijeko to get there first.

After the seniority of the age mates had been established by the race, Kiserian and the other initiate girls, each carrying a freshly cut branch from the mugumo tree, walked single file down a path to the clan's river. Younger children lined the path, mocking the initiates and shouting insults at them. It was the last time that the girls would have to tolerate the foolish teasing of childhood.

The girls walked into the water, deep enough to cover

their genital areas, and then stood there, allowing the numbing cold to anesthetize them for their cutting. One at a time, the girls threw the branches into the river and watched the current carry them around the corner and out of sight. Childhood disappeared with the branches.

Soon the girls heard women singing under a mugumo tree across the river. Silently they crossed to the other side and walked past the quiet, respectful faces of the same children who had mocked them just minutes before. The initiates went to the base of the mugumo tree, surrounded by the women of the clan, and sat down close together in a line. Behind each girl sat their mentor, who locked them into position for the cutting.

***

Kiserian was second in the line of eight girls sitting on a soft bed of mugumo leaves under the giant branches of the tree. The morning had started with nine girls, but an odd number of initiates would invite a curse from an angry ancestor, and so one was sent home and told to return when the season for cutting came again. Kiserian knew she could have gotten to the mugumo tree first, but she was certain that she did not yet know enough about Gikuyu customs to be the leader of the initiates after circumcision. It seemed clear to Kiserian that Kijeko was a natural leader and that it was a great honor for her friend to go first. Along with winning the right to be the leader, Kijeko had also won the right to be the first to be cut. Kiserian would be second.

The surgeon was dressed in finely cured goatskins dyed red. Her head covering was made from the black-and-white skin of the colobus monkey, and her face and arms were bright white from a mixture of sheep fat and mukuyu ashes.

As the surgeon knelt down and placed her knife between Kijeko's legs, the woman holding the young girl in position burst out in song. Then Kijeko's mother and relatives joined in the singing with loud voices and sharp staccato clapping. They sang of how Ngai had given Gikuyu women to be the owners of the household and the givers of life, of how they were all children of the first Gikuyu woman, Mumbai, who was fashioned from the flesh of Ngai.

"My child, once the surgeon begins, she will move quickly down the line," Kiserian's mentor told her quietly.

Kiserian nodded and glanced at the girls sitting to her left and then at Kijeko. She watched as Kijeko's eyes widened with fear and anticipation. Kiserian could see that her friend was about to lose control.

The woman behind Kijeko clasped her hands around the girl's eyes and pulled her head back against the woman's breasts. Kiserian fought the urge to look away as the surgeon reached between her friend's legs. She could see the girl twitch and cry out, but the singing and clapping drowned out the sound. The surgeon took the soft cloth draped on the girl's leg, put soft-pulped aloe on it, and pressed it onto the wound. The woman behind took her hands off the girl's face and reached down to hold the cloth. Kijeko looked at Kiserian. Her dark eyes stared like a goat in the throes of death.

The surgeon quickly moved and placed her instrument between Kiserian's legs. The young girl caught the surgeon's eye and managed a smile.

"You are a brave one, my child," the surgeon said.

The chorus of songs burst out behind Kiserian. The surgeon looked at the old woman holding her and nodded to indicate that it was time to cover the girl's eyes. Both Kiserian and her mentor shook their heads. The young girl glanced back at Kijeko and their eyes met again. Kiserian refocused and forced herself to watch as the surgeon pushed back her vulva, and then set her teeth in anticipation as the woman pinched the edge of her clitoris between her fingers and cut off its tip. Kiserian's body arced backwards as she felt the searing cut of the knife, and her body shuddered under the white-hot flames of pain.

She forced herself to look down again and watch as the surgeon grabbed first one and then the other tip of her

95

labia and cut them off as well. The excruciating pain from her severed clitoris blocked any further pain she might have felt from the two remaining cuts.

The surgeon placed the leaves and cloth on the wound. She took a decorated skin blanket and wrapped it around Kiserian and under her arms and then pressed the young girl's knees together and glanced up at her face. Kiserian was barely conscious but felt herself smile. She had practiced that smile for many weeks. The surgeon nodded and the women's singing burst into cheers. This one, they said to each other, was more than a Gikuyu woman; she was surely a leader of her age mates, and she was the one the young warriors would want to dance with.

Kiserian shivered uncontrollably. She turned her head and once again met the eyes of her friend. It was clear that, even in her suffering, Kijeko was impressed by Kiserian's act of defiance against fear and pain. Kiserian did not care so much whether her act of bravery would attract the attention of her age mates, or the warriors at the dances. But she hoped that Shushu Njoki's son, Waitimu, would hear of her feat.

SHADOWS

Ma'muriuki and her children stepped out of the veil of trees that surrounded the okijabe and worked their way down the gentle slope that marked the boundary between the Gikuyu highlands and the Maasai grasslands. In front of them rose the Mountain of Boys, an easy day's journey away. In the distance, beyond the golden savannah grass, were the Mountain of Jagged Edges and the hazy purple outline of the Mountain of Spirits. Both were formed when Enkai was angry and sent hot rocks filled with fire to warn the Maasai.

Ma'muriuki pointed to the small mountain. "We will go to the side of the Mountain of Boys where the sun still shines. There we will spend our first night in the lands of the Maasai."

"Mama, I have learned only to despise the Maasai. We do not allow Maasai to come on our lands. How will we live in their lands?" Wangari spat on the ground in disgust.

"I was once a Maasai. It is not good to despise these people, my daughter. Their ways are not like ours, but in the eyes of Ngai, they are still our brothers."

"How are they our brothers, Mama, when they steal from us?" Wangari asked.

"Do you remember the story of the three brothers, my

child? This story is told by both the Maasai and the Gikuyu people," Ma'muriuki said.

"I do not know this story, Mama."

"Listen, then. It is important that you always remember this story. There was a man who lived on the earth who had three sons. His sons constantly quarreled with each other. Their constant fighting distressed the father, so he took his sons to the holy mountain to ask Ngai, the creator of all things, for advice.

"Ngai placed a spear, a digging stick, and a bow on the ground in front of the sons and told each brother to choose one.

"One son chose the spear. He was sent to the savannah plains and told to be a great warrior and to be the father of the Maasai, who keep livestock on the earth.

"The second son chose the bow. He was sent to the forests and told that he and his children would be the N'dorobo, hunters of animals.

"The last son chose the digging stick. He was told to till the earth and build shambas. He would be the father of the Gikuyu and all those who live from the crops of the field.

"So the three brothers went their separate ways and had many children. Though they quarreled at times, they always remained brothers, and they remembered that they came from the same father."

Ma'muriuki bent down, gently put a hand on the shoulder of each daughter, and turned them to face her. "Always remember this story, my children. We are not the enemy of the Maasai. The Gikuyu and the Maasai are quarreling brothers, but they have the same father."

She straightened and began to lead the way across the savannah. The stale-sweet smell of the tall golden grass triggered a distant memory in her, a childhood memory of pulling the grass and chewing on the sweet ends while she was moving cattle. She smiled and glanced at her children. The world they knew was made only of shambas and forests; the world that they now entered had neither. She wondered if she would be able to introduce her children to their new world with the same skill that her shushu used in showing the Gikuyu world to her.

"Mama, what are these strange wooden shapes on the ground?" Wangari pointed at a curved piece of wood. The young girl bent down and reached for it.

"Don't touch it!" Ma'muriuki warned. "Let me try to understand what it is first."

She stooped down next to her child and examined the odd object. The outside shape was a circular piece of wood surrounded by what appeared to be metal, like a spear. In the middle was a much smaller wooden circle with pieces of wood evenly connecting the outside circle to the inside one. It was obvious to her that the object was man-made, but try as she might, she could not recall any object like it from her Maasai childhood.

"Mama," Wangari said. "It looks like the shape of the moon."

"Butterfly People!" Ma'muriuki said. She grabbed her girls and pulled them away from the object. "Children, this is what made the marks in the trail that we saw with the trader women."

"How does it walk, Mama?"

"I do not have an answer for you, my child, but this one appears to be broken. Perhaps the Butterfly People made another one to replace it," Ma'muriuki said. "We must be very careful. The world here is not the same as when I was a child."

"It is different because there are Butterfly People," Wangari said.

Ma'muriuki took her daughters by the hand and led them around the strange object. She redirected them toward the little mountain ahead and resumed walking. It was becoming clear that other things were different about the savannah lands. The telltale signs of the Maasai people were missing. The Maasai usually made controlled burns across the savannah lands to encourage new grass growth for their cattle and make it easier to spot predators. But the savannah grasses that Ma'muriuki and her children walked through were tall, and the crisscrosses of trails left by the Maasai cattle were missing. It was as if no Maasai had lived in the area for a long time.

The mother kept her children close beside her as she walked, keeping a constant lookout for signs of movement in the grasses. Her vigilance paid off when she caught sight of a dark shadow, which seemed to appear and disappear. She knew at once that a lion had spotted them.

"My children, we will stop here to rest," the mother said.

"But Mama, we have not walked far," Wangari said.

"Sit, children." Her daughters immediately obeyed. She cinched the sleeping Maathai tighter on her back.

Ma'muriuki began to sing in Maasai. It was a song her children had never heard before. She broke off a thin branch from a small bush and split it into small sticks about the length of her hand. She bent down and placed a stick between each of her daughters' toes, covering their mouths to indicate they should be quiet. She stood up and began braiding sections of the tall savannah grasses together until her children were surrounded by the braided stalks. Then she sat down next to her children and put sticks between her own toes. She lifted her hands up and began to chant in Maasai. Finally, she stopped and put her arms around her girls.

"Rest now, children." She smiled at them.

"Is it a buffalo, Mama?" Wangari asked.

"We are safe, child. Ngai will protect us." Wangari looked at her mother's face and then nodded and soon fell asleep with her sister. Ma'muriuki decided the explanation of her actions should wait until the lingering shadow a few feet away disappeared.

DANCE

"Hurry, my friend, I want to find a good man before you do. *One cannot get warm from a fire unless they stir the embers,*" Kijeko said. She watched with impatient exasperation as Kiserian rubbed the bright red mixture of sheep fat and red ochre on her shoulders and neck.

The hut was an open, undivided space serving as the temporary living quarters for the same eight young women who had been cut together six months before. All were now healed enough to start attending the dances. They traveled together from clan to clan and would continue to do so for several years. Their hair had not grown back enough to begin plaiting it like that of the older girls at the dance. But being younger was not a disadvantage, as many of the older girls who were still dancing had either found a partner they were getting to know or had not yet been picked by a warrior.

"The man I will marry is not dancing tonight," Kiserian said. She handed the mixture to her friend and sat on the stool beside her. "But you will fix my head, too, because I must dance with many men to show my resolve to wait."

"I do not understand who you wait for, my friend; all the warriors want to dance with you. They say of you, *She is one whose beauty itches.* There are more for you to choose from than there are for me."

"But my shushu reminds me that *beauty alone does no man good*," Kiserian said. "I cannot speak of my intentions because I do not want to bring a bad omen upon myself for speaking of the future as if I have heard instructions from Ngai."

"Then you should not dance," Kijeko said, "and I can get more warriors to dance with me."

"Ah! But my friend," Kiserian said, "when I dance with a warrior, I whisper your praises in his ear and tell him of your bravery at the cutting. Besides, I must dance at every dance, because I do not know when the hand I wait for will be waiting for me. I will not stand between you and any warrior."

Kijeko motioned that she was finished with Kiserian's head and the young women exchanged places.

"You should know that there are things said about you," Kijeko said.

"Tell me, my friend, if you wish," Kiserian replied.

"It is said among the warriors that if you do not accept the hand on your shoulder soon, they will decide that you are no longer one to dance with."

"This is a hard thing for me to decide," Kiserian said. "If I stand on the feet of a warrior, I will give hope to someone that I know will not be returned. But if I do not, then it will be as you say, and I will not be dancing when the one I wait for appears."

"Then you should stand on the feet of a warrior, but do not give him hope for more than one night. That is my advice. If I see you dancing on the feet of a warrior, it would give me hope too."

"But if I give a warrior hope for the one night when the one I wait for appears, then he will think that I have found another."

Kijeko laughed. "You think too much, my friend. But listen to me. If the one you wait for is not among the warriors, then he will not come to the dances during the first season. The first season is for the senior warriors to find wives. During your second or third season, that is when those who are no longer warriors and are working their shambas will come to the dance."

Kiserian finished decorating her friend's face with ochre and white ash. "You look like a true Gikuyu woman ready to find her warrior. Now, let me think about your advice while you get me ready for the dance." She sat on the wooden stool while her friend mixed more ash and ochre to make some final touches. It suddenly occurred to Kiserian that the other girls were not talking and had been listening to her conversation.

"Listen to me, my friend," Kiserian said. "I was born of the Maasai, and while I have learned many things, I do not know all the ways of the Gikuyu. I did not know that a person who is not still a warrior would wait until after the first season to come to the dance. Do you speak for all my age mates here when you say it would be better for me to stand on the feet of a warrior from time to time?"

"Yes, my friend. You were the bravest at the cuttings, and it is our custom that you choose first. We would insult you if we chose first. You have earned this privilege."

"I do not understand. You were the chosen one, which is why you were cut first," Kiserian said.

"But you took my place when you showed no fear or pain at the cutting." Kijeko began to retouch the red mixture around Kiserian's head and forehead. "It is you, not me, that is the leader in this hut."

"I did not mean to take what belongs to you," Kiserian said. "I did not know that another could take your place as the leader. I am deeply sorry for doing that."

The girls in the hut laughed along with Kijeko.

"My friend, what happened is what should happen. But you should know that it is the girls in the other huts who are stepping on the feet of the warriors. We wait for you."

"Hurry up then, my friend," Kiserian said. "Today, I will step on the feet of the first warrior who puts his hand on my shoulder. I will not be the cause of all of you becoming second wives after the warriors have made their choices."

***

Kiserian stepped into the hut with the warrior close behind her. She waited briefly while her eyes adjusted to the smoky darkness. She saw that nearly all the girls were already lying next to warriors on the leaf-covered ground.

"Come over here, my friend, and take this space next to us," Kijeko said.

Kiserian and her companion stepped their way between and over the other couples as they followed Kijeko's voice to the open space she held for them.

"You painted my face well," Kijeko said. "I have found a strong warrior to keep me warm tonight."

Kiserian's friend sat naked save for the tightly secured sheepskin wrapped from below her navel to her upper thighs. The warrior was gently stroking the small soft rounds of her breasts. He looked up and nodded pleasantly to Kiserian and her companion.

Kiserian smiled and stood hesitantly. She did not know for certain what she was supposed to do next. She had not been touched by a boy since she was a Maasai girl, when it was normal for the young boys and girls to explore each other physically. The Gikuyu taboo against genital contact among the unmarried still confused her. But she was proud of how her breasts were developing, and she felt a stirring desire to have them touched by a warrior.

"You are a beautiful woman," her companion said. "It is said that I am the first warrior whose feet you have stepped on." As he spoke, he reached around her from behind and unwrapped the soft covering over her breasts. She did not know what to do in response, so she looked at him and tried to smile encouragement at his action. He reached down and removed the lower wrap around her waist. She stood naked except for the white cloth wrapped tightly around her thighs and waist. The warrior then took off his waistcloth, revealing his own bound midsection. He sat on the leaves and reached up his hand to draw Kiserian down with him. "Come sit with me and tell me why I am so honored, if indeed, I am the first."

Kiserian glanced at Kijeko, who was hiding a smile. Clearly, she was eager to hear how her friend was going to answer that question.

"I am in my first season of dancing," Kiserian said. "I have many seasons ahead to choose a man for marriage. Perhaps, if I dance well, the man Ngai has for me will be among the dancers. You are right, you are first, but it is up to Ngai to decide how many other dances and seasons there must be."

"I see you choose words carefully. That is a good thing for someone who will one day be a giver of life among the Gikuyu," he said.

The couples in the hut settled down to whispering and soft laughter. Kiserian learned of her suitor's clan and family. He was from an Anjiur subclan. When she told him she was from the Angari clan, they both agreed that their parents would approve of a marriage between them. He seemed pleased that he had found a girl his parents would accept. Kiserian was pleased that she had found a warrior her friend lying next to her could accept. She leaned into her suitor and whispered, "You are a good man, and I hear that you are a strong warrior. I am pleased that I have found you. However, you should know that it is not my time yet to find a mate. I have many seasons ahead. But my friend, Kijeko, is also from my clan. She is hunting for a warrior."

His eyes widened slightly in response to her forthright manner. His hand fell away from her breasts as he tried to make sense of her statement. "I will not be the one who will win your affection? I do not understand why you stepped on my feet. *There is no good affection between a leopard and a goat.*"

Kiserian took his hand and pressed it back onto her breast. "I do not refuse you, but at tomorrow's dance, if I do not step on your feet, it is not because you have not pleased me tonight but because my time for choosing has not come. I do not refuse you, but I am still young. Tonight, I am happy that I am with a warrior like you. We should enjoy this, and I want to learn more of your accomplishments since you have been a warrior."

"So you will learn of my accomplishments, and then you will not stand on my feet again?"

"I will not step on your feet again unless you understand that I do so because I think you are a good suitor, but I am not ready to be a wife. If you understand this, then I will step on your feet from time to time, and you can try to win my affection. But you would become angry if you did not understand my intentions first."

"No woman has ever told me this," the warrior said. He did not seem angry, which was a great relief to Kiserian. "If I put my hand on your shoulder, would you let me try to win you to me, or would you refuse me even that?"

"Oh, my warrior friend, if you can win me to you, then I would be happy, but you should know that I am hoping for another to come to the dances and put his hand on my shoulder. If you can make me forget about him, then you will have won me. But listen to me: my friend Kijeko lies with a warrior next to us. She was a mighty person at our cutting. She was the first to reach the mugumo tree and the first to be cut under the tree."

"But the word among the warriors is that you are the one who showed no fear, and it is you who became the leader among the girls in your hut."

"I did not show my pain, but I should not be the leader, as even now it is the other girls who are teaching me the ways of the Gikuyu."

"It is your modesty that makes you a leader, and it is your modesty that will keep you a leader among the Gikuyu. There is no higher value."

"Then perhaps I should stand up now and boast to everyone in the hut that I am the greatest. Maybe then they will see someone else as the true leader."

"If you do not want to be the leader, then you should stand up and boast. I do not think you will, because such boasting is not part of your nature, and even if you did such a foolish thing, everyone would see right through it." The warrior stroked her stomach and leaned in and took her nipple between his teeth and gently pulled. He watched with satisfaction as her nipple responded to his play. "You are one who could satisfy a man. I hear that you work hard in the shamba of your shushu."

"All girls work hard in the shamba, which is what Ngai has given us to do. You please me with your mouth, but look beyond me to the breast of my friend. She is satisfying her warrior with breasts that are bigger than mine. You should put your hand on her shoulder at the next dance and learn if my words are not true for yourself."

"I will consider your friend at the next dance, but tonight I will consider only you."

Kiserian sighed and nodded. She placed her hands along his strong arms.

THE MAASAI TRAIL

Ma'muriuki stopped under the shade of a lone acacia tree and carefully looked in every direction. There was a time when she would have needed little more than a glance to spot danger, but that seemed like a lifetime ago. She looked at every bush and tree to catch the dark shade of a lion's back or the black outline of a lone buffalo, but she saw no sign of danger. She had not seen any signs of the Butterfly People since the day before. At last, she decided the place was safe enough. "We will rest here, my children."

The girls' steps had become sluggish. They were not accustomed to the acacia root and bitter herb soup she gave them, and they only bravely tried to drink it.

"Mama, why are there no shambas here? How do Maasai people eat food without shambas?" Wangari asked.

Ma'muriuki smiled. She was not much older than her daughter when she was introduced to new customs herself. "My daughter, the Maasai do not have shambas. They eat from the roots of plants and from the blood and meat of their animals. They eat some Gikuyu food, because our traders barter it with them, but we have no need for Maasai food, so it is strange to you. You will soon learn that their food can still keep you strong."

"Mama, the shamba is the work of women. What does a Maasai woman do, then?"

"Maasai women think that Gikuyu women work too hard. But they also have work. They build the houses in the manyatta and inspect the condition of the livestock, and they make the food from milk, blood, and root plants for their families."

"Mama, the roots make my stomach hurt, and they do not satisfy my hunger."

"I know, my child. Soon we will be in a manyatta, and you will eat other food that will make your stomach hurt even more. But you will get used to it, and your stomach will not hurt as much then."

Wangari's face twisted in a show of disgust. "But, Mama, you have taught us that the blessings of Ngai come from our hard work and bringing good crops from the shamba. Is this why the Maasai need our food so often, because they are too lazy?"

"The Maasai follow the ways of Enkai, who teaches them that their blessings come from their cattle and the fearlessness of their morani. The Gikuyu look down on the Maasai, but they admire their skills as warriors, and the Maasai look down on the Gikuyu, but they admire our skills as traders. But my daughter should know that there have been some very great wars against others who wanted to drive us from our lands or take our people as slaves. In those wars, the Maasai and the Gikuyu made strong allies, and we have kept each other's borders safe."

"Mama, I think the Maasai are disgusting and lazy people."

Ma'muriuki laughed, startling her children. She had not laughed in a long time, and it was infectious. Even little Maathai giggled. "My child, I was only a little younger than you when I said the same thing about the Gikuyu."

Wangari stopped laughing. "Mama, do I have to become a Maasai now?"

Makena grew serious and leaned next to her older sister, waiting to hear their mother's answer.

"My child, there was no one who made me become a Gikuyu. I had to choose for myself. I will never tell you to become a Maasai, but if you choose to do so, I will not prevent you from making this choice."

"Mama, will you become a Maasai again?"

"I do not know, my child," Ma'muriuki said. "No more questions for now. Do not wander beyond the shade of this tree. You do not yet know the ways of the Maasai lands. We will begin again when I have rested and, perhaps, if Ngai is kind, we will find a manyatta before the sun hides from us."

***

"Mama!"

Ma'muriuki shook herself awake. She jumped up from the base of the tree in panic, gazing from Makena's pointing arm to an ostrich running full speed toward Wangari, who carried a large ostrich egg in her arms. Unaware, she was walking slowly just beyond the shade of the tree.

"Child, drop that and run to me, quickly!"

Hearing the alarm in her mother's voice, Wangari dropped the egg and ran. Ma'muriuki scooped up Makena and lifted her onto the lowest branch of the tree. "Climb higher, my child, and wait for Wangari to hand Maathai to you." She turned just in time to scoop up Wangari from her run and set her beside her sister. "Take Maathai, child, and get higher up the tree with your brother and sister." Ma'muriuki could hear the thundering gait of the ostrich behind her and breathed a prayer that the angry hen was alone.

She took off running to a tree fifty steps away, waving her arms and shouting loudly. Ma'muriuki glanced over her shoulder and saw that the bird had changed direction, quickly closing in on her. She grabbed a thick branch on the ground and broke it across her knee, fashioning a makeshift club. She had no chance of reaching the tree.

Two warthogs, drawn by her shouting, charged out of their den in fright. They sped across the grasslands in front of her. Ma'muriuki turned sharply and jumped into the creatures' den. She worked her way backwards into the long,

110

narrow hole that angled deep into the earth, beyond the reach of the ostrich's deadly claws. The angry hen dug around the surface of the hole, trying to reach her. Each time it dipped its head into the hole, Ma'muriuki swung at it with her club, and each time it squawked and returned to its digging.

Ma'muriuki felt something wiggling behind her feet and realized that the escaping warthogs had left their litter of piglets in the den. The frightened boar and sow had run away to distract the attacker from their young. They would soon return, determined to protect their own.

One does not fear the warthog unless one is down a warthog hole. Ma'muriuki heard the trampling sounds of the ostrich running and the screaming snorts of the warthogs in hot pursuit. She popped out of the hole and watched them chase the big bird right under the tree where her children were perched and out into the open grasses beyond. She ran to the tree.

"Are you safe, my children?" she asked, gazing upward.

"Yes, Mama," Wangari said. "We thought the ostrich was killing you."

"I am safe, child." Ma'muriuki was too relieved to be angry with Wangari. "You children stay in that tree until we know if the ostrich will forget about us."

The warthogs grew tired of the chase and returned to their hole. The ostrich turned back and charged the hogs, but they whirled around and chased off the bird once more. The two girls giggled at the spectacle. Ma'muriuki looked around and did not see any other ostriches. She retrieved the egg Wangari had dropped and inspected it; the tough shell was unbroken by the fall. She brought it back to the base of the tree. "Tell me if the ostrich comes back," she said.

She cracked the egg with her makeshift club, peeled off the top few inches of broken shell, and poked through the membrane with her stick, mixing the large yoke and white together. When she was satisfied, she took a deep drink of the liquid. After glancing around and seeing no sign of the ostrich, she carefully set the egg upright between some rocks and called her children to come down and join her. The girls handed Maathai to her as she helped them down.

"Drink from the shell quickly, my children. We must leave before the mother realizes that we are still near her eggs." They took turns drinking the liquid. Ma'muriuki spit portions into Maathai's mouth. "This will keep us strong until we find a manyatta."

Makena was still excited about the ostrich and repeated what had happened over and over. Wangari grew quiet. She had not stayed in the shade as her mother instructed and had nearly gotten them all killed. This was the second time that she had put everyone in danger by not listening to her mother. She waited to hear what her mother would say.

There was too much of the ostrich egg for them to drink in one sitting. Ma'muriuki poured as much of the remaining contents into her empty cooking gourd as she could, knowing it would not last long and that they would have to drink it soon or pour it out before it hardened and ruined the gourd. The remaining fluid was left in the shell for some lucky scavenger to finish up. Ma'muriuki tied Maathai onto her back and motioned for her girls to follow.

By now, the Mountain of Boys had disappeared behind the spirit mountain, Ol Doinyo Nyokie. They were near the place where her childhood home had been. It seemed strange to her that in the journey so far, she had not seen a single manyatta. She wondered if the Maasai had moved farther away because of the Butterfly People. She looked back to make certain the ostrich was not following them and caught sight of a short line of moran warriors approaching from the side. The glint of their spears and the deep red ochre dye on their long braided hair left little doubt who they were. It was the moment Ma'muriuki had both feared and hoped for.

"Children, you must listen to my voice and do what I say." The girls nodded. "Wangari, you have not listened to my voice twice, but Ngai has spared us. This time, if you do not listen to me, Ngai may give up on you and take us to be with him,. Do you understand?"

"Mama, I am sorry…"

"Quiet, child. It is a thing already forgotten, but you must listen this time."

"Yes, Mama."

"My children, we are soon to meet some morani. These are great warriors among the Maasai people. If they accept us as Maasai, we will be safe, but if they believe we are Gikuyu, it will not go well for us. When I speak to them, you will not speak and you will not show them any disrespect. Do you hear me?"

"I hear you, Mama," Wangari said.

Makena nodded but said nothing. She took the hand of her big sister and moved closer to her mother.

"Come, then, let us meet these warriors and learn from them," Ma'muriuki said. They walked to a large grove of acacia trees and waited for the morani there, out of the midday sun. The mother instructed her girls to sit against the tree and handed Maathai to them. She gave them a drink of the thickening egg mixture and then sat between the girls and the approaching men, remembering that her mother had never stood to greet a Maasai warrior.

She counted five of them. From their appearance, she decided that they were slightly older, perhaps even her age. They would not be as hotheaded as younger warriors trying to prove themselves and, perhaps, would be better acquainted with her clan.

They arrived at the perimeter of the trees. Four of them stopped and faced in different directions. They planted their spears in the ground and stood on one leg, with the other leg wrapped around the shaft of the spear. The fifth warrior approached her. She could see the crisscross of scars on his bare shoulders and chest. His long, braided red hair was tightly woven. She knew then that they were not far from a manyatta.

"*Soba*," the warrior said.

"*Eego*," she said, giving the female reply to a warrior's greeting.

The man stood quietly, looking at Ma'muriuki and the girls. He seemed in no hurry to speak.

"Let us speak together," she said. "I do not know if I should address you as my child or my brother." Ma'muriuki picked up her gourd. "This is from the egg of an ostrich; I must throw it out soon before it ruins my gourd. It is the only thing I have to offer the warrior and his clansmen."

The man took the gourd from her outstretched hand and sipped. He turned and motioned to one of the other warriors to come take the gourd and then motioned for him to pass it around. He turned and faced her again.

"We watched to see if you were a Maasai woman or Gikuyu," he said. "Your dress like a Gikuyu, and you carry your child like a Gikuyu, but you showed Maasai skill with the ostrich, and you speak our language."

"My father was a leader of warriors and a spiritual man that they called a *laibon*. My mother called him Naengop. He was from the Ildamat clan, of the House of the Red Oxen. When I last saw them, we lived in a manyatta near here. I am looking for my clan to learn if any of my relatives still live. You can decide for yourself if I am a Maasai."

"You speak the Maasai tongue well. You have not forgotten your clan. I will not judge if you are Maasai. That is for your clan to decide. I have heard of your father, but I know that he was given to the hyenas when I was young. My manyatta was once one of the Ildamat, but there were too few of us that survived the wrath of Nanyoki. Those who remained in my manyatta joined the Ilkisongo clan, but we are also of the House of the Red Oxen."

"I wonder if there is one who may know if any from my manyatta still live and where they may be now." Ma'muriuki did not show any reaction to the offhand manner in which the moran informed her of her father's death. But, then, there had been no doubt in her mind that the wasted figure she last saw could not have survived long.

The warrior pointed to a small clump of acacia trees. "Does the daughter of Naengop the great *laibon* see those three trees standing together?"

Ma'muriuki stood and looked quietly in that direction until she agreed that she knew which trees he was pointing out to her.

"You should go toward those trees, but before you get there, you will see the markings of many cows. If you wait at those markings, the young boys of our manyatta will be going along that path soon, and you can follow them to our manyatta. There are men there who will know where those from your clans may be reached."

"May Enkai bless you for your kindness to a Maasai woman," Ma'muriuki said.

The warrior laughed. "Nanyoki would show his face if I did not respect a woman. Our people have seen enough of the angry face of Enkai. But I think I have heard that sons of the great Naengop are in the lands near the Mountain of Narok, in the place called Seyabei. It may be that your relatives are not far beyond our manyatta. But if they are your brothers, they too are no longer a part of the Ildamat clan."

"You have given me news that is good," Ma'muriuki said. "I will gather my children and go to the path for cattle that you speak of. Peace to your family." She tilted her head slightly and briefly placed her right hand over her left breast.

The warrior returned the gesture. "The daughter of Naengop should know that my clan is permitted to marry the daughters of the Ildamat clans. You are still of breeding age. If there is no spear planted outside your door at the manyatta tonight, it may be that I will plant mine at your door."

She had long forgotten about the morani and their spears. When she was a child, it was common for a warrior to stab a spear into the ground at the entrance of her mother's house. There had been one lover her mother especially liked who was a warrior under her father. Her father was eager for her mother to have a child with the warrior, because he believed the warrior would plant good seed in her mother and give her father strong sons.

Among the Gikuyu, it was also acceptable for a husband

to allow one of his wives to accept one of his age mates into her hut. But this was not common among the Gikuyu and rarely talked about openly. For such favors, an age mate would usually have to exchange a goat with the husband. On Ma'muriuki's part, she did not know of any girls among her age mates who had been a part of such an agreement.

Among the Maasai, the warrior only had to plant his spear in front of the woman's enkaji as a sign to other warriors that the woman was busy.

"The leader among warriors would be welcome to come and spend the night, but my legs will not open until I am free from my obligations and my age set is established," Ma'muriuki said.

She could, according to Maasai custom, take a warrior in her husband's age set, but she did not have a Maasai husband, and she was not yet ready to become a full Maasai again. She could not bring herself to sever her ties with the Gikuyu. She remembered the words of the medicine man: One day, Muriuki would return honor to her and her family. Becoming a true Maasai might end her hope that the words of the medicine man would come true.

The warrior nodded in an understanding way. "I will wait until the daughter of Naengop has found her relatives and has an enkaji of her own to live in. It may be on that day that she is ready for the seed of a warrior."

Without saying another word, the warrior turned and walked back in the direction that the men had come from. "*Soba!*" the men called out to Ma'muriuki as they turned and followed their leader.

"*Eego,*" Ma'muriuki responded. She motioned for her children to follow her in the direction of the trees and the cattle trail. She hoped it would lead to the end of her journey.

WARRIORS AND FARMERS

The Gikuyu clans took turns hosting the dances between the warriors and the newly initiated women. The dances took place on the lands of the wealthy, and each host tried to outdo the others in attracting as many dancers as possible. It was one of the primary ways that the clans, often many days' journey away from each other, stayed interconnected. Wives and shushus cooked sweet yams and prepared bitter gruel while butchers roasted goat meat for the crowds. Old men sat in circles outside the dance area drinking honey beer. Everyone sang rhythmically and clapped along with the drummers as they watched the dancing.

Kiserian learned that she could stand on the feet of a warrior every three or four dances without raising suspicion. She began to see herself as a matchmaker for her hut. Spending a night with a warrior, she would determine his eligibility with her clan and push him onto the girls she felt most likely to be his match.

If the girls knew what she was doing, they said nothing. But she did find matches for several of them, and the warriors, at least, seemed grateful to her. She remained the leader for almost two full seasons, no matter how hard she lobbied for her friend Kijeko to retake the leadership.

117

But Kijeko had found a warrior who pleased her, and at every dance the warrior would put his hand on her shoulder, and she would step on his feet, and more often than not, they would stop abruptly and walk to the hut before the first song ended.

***

It was on one of the clan hilltops far from Kiserian's home that the dance was interrupted by the plaintive ululation of war. The high-pitched cry carried from hilltop to hilltop, alerting the Gikuyu of a Maasai raid on a neighboring clan. The warriors disappeared into the woods, carrying the spears and shields they had left at the edge of the dancing circle. The girls and musicians hesitated briefly before running into the woods on the other side of the clearing. A few stayed behind to help the elderly and the children into the shelter of the trees. Most buried themselves under leaves and branches, while a few of the younger elders stood at the edge of the woods, watching for signs of danger and waiting to hear news from other elders. All harbored a great fear of the brooding spirits that lingered in the shadows at night, but at the first sounds of war, they did not hesitate to bury themselves in the safety of those same dark shadows.

Shrill war cries broke long periods of silence. It seemed that the fighting was taking place along the hillside of the clan on the next ridge, but no messenger came that night to tell them it was safe. They stayed silent; mothers struggled to keep their babies warm and stifled their cries with soft whispers in their ears.

Kiserian loathed these Maasai invaders. She had once been proud of the moran fighters returning to the manyatta with the cows or goats that they had taken victoriously from their Gikuyu neighbors. But what she once thought of as an act of bravery, she now regarded as theft. The Gikuyu rarely raided the Maasai, except to take back possessions that the Maasai had first seized from them, plus compensation for their losses. What she had seen as a child as Gikuyu cowardice, she now saw as honorable.

She stood up quietly and walked to the forest's edge, to the side of a young elder. He seemed startled to see her there.

"Does the young woman not hear that there is fighting still, and yet she does not hide under the shadows of the ancestors?"

"I have no fear of the fighting," Kiserian said truthfully. "I do not understand what I hear or how the Gikuyu fight when the Maasai take their animals."

The elder stared thoughtfully at Kiserian then said, "The Maasai are fierce warriors. We try not to fight with them in open battle, unless there is no other way.. When they raid us to steal our cattle, we do not help the clan that is being attacked."

"Then will the Maasai kill them?"

"Some of them will die, but most will escape unharmed. The Maasai are not after the Gikuyu, they are after our livestock. The clan under attack will not fight them directly, but they will try to delay the invaders' escape with our animals."

"Why do they delay the Maasai if there is no one to help fight them?"

"The warriors from the other clans go to the Maasai escape routes and set war-pits and traps so that the Maasai will not get away easily. A few Gikuyu warriors will die, but many more Maasai morani will die in their attempt to take our livestock from our lands. Once they give up our cattle and goats, we will let the rest of them go back to their homeland. We have many relatives among the Maasai. We defend what is ours, but we do not wish them harm."

"I was once a child among the Maasai," Kiserian said, "but I am thankful to Ngai for allowing me to be counted among your people."

"I understand now why you have no fear," he said. "Your first birth was among a fierce people."

"When we are traveling between clans for the dances," she said, "I have been shown how to recognize war-pits and avoid them, but I have never looked into one to see what was in it."

"My child, a war-pit is a dangerous thing. It is a hole with many sharpened stakes pointing up from the bottom. When a person falls into one, they do not often live. It is good to avoid them. Strong branches cover the holes so that one can walk over them with little danger. Even the Maasai raiders walk over them and do not know what is beneath their feet. However, when they return from their raids, we remove the strong branches and replace them with weak ones. There is the blood of many morani in those war-pits."

"Tonight the sounds of the war come from different places," Kiserian said.

"We have a saying: *Disunited* morani *can be beaten with one club*. Our warriors try to force the Maasai warriors to divide and escape in different directions. They then set their traps for the smaller bands and finish them. Soon the morani will lose their will to fight and let go of our animals. What you have heard are sounds of success from our warriors. The fighting is almost over. The Maasai were very foolish to raid this far into our lands. We have many traps waiting for them along their way home."

"Then can you tell me why we are still hiding?"

"You ask many questions," the elder said. He chuckled to show her he was not displeased. "Your mother must have grown tired of you."

"My shushu is my mother, and she tells me that I must never stop asking questions."

"You have a wise shushu. Here is the answer to your question. The Maasai understand our ways, as we understand theirs. Sometimes they will send small groups of morani to surrounding Gikuyu clans to attack them and divide our warriors. When we hear the sounds of war, we all hide so they have no one to attack. Those of us elders who are still young can fight as well as the warriors, so we stay and defend our people. This fight is over, and I do not think there is any other danger for us, but we will wait to hear that it is safe to return to our huts."

At first light, a loud, musical ululation erupted from the southern hilltops. Almost instantly, the same musical shouting came from the woods behind Kiserian, sending the message to clans on ridges further north.

The young elder stood up and motioned for her to follow him as people emerged from the woods. "Now, when the warriors return, we will hear about their victories," he said. "Some young warriors have made themselves leaders today, and others will want to hide from the world. *Just because one has been to war, it does not mean they have been in battle.*"

The clearing became busy with activity. Kiserian and the young women from her hut joined the older women in pounding the sugar cane into juice for honey beer, while young women from other huts joined in the food preparations.

Young boys led goats to the butchers, who quickly prepared them for a victory celebration. The women cooks placed large clay pots filled with blood and juices from the goats on the fires and stuffed the emptied stomachs with cuttings of meat, yams, and arrowroots to be boiled for hours. The goat heads set directly on the fire were rotated over the coals until they turned black. Young girls took knives and scraped off the singed hairs until their mothers decided that the heads were clean enough to be boiled for soup.

Kiserian paused from pounding sugar cane while the older woman next to her took her turn. She looked around the clearing at the scurry of people: everyone, old and young alike, moved efficiently from task to task without taking or giving instructions.

Another woman came and stood next to her. "Does the young woman have a warrior that she waits for?"

Kiserian looked at the woman for a moment, and then a slight smile crept over her face. "No. I still wait to dance with the one with whom my heart is mended. I was once a child of the Maasai and was taught the Gikuyu women worked like beasts of burden. But now I see a people who work hard and rarely lack food. I know now that it is the Maasai who suffer because they do not like work. *Idleness is the road of the beggar.* They are too proud to work, and yet the Gikuyu are too proud not to work. *In hard work, one finds no shame.* My Maasai mother told my shushu that I would become a hard worker and a good Gikuyu woman. I was ashamed of my first mother's words to my shushu. Now I am proud of them."

"You are a good Gikuyu woman." The old woman put her hand on Kiserian's shoulder and smiled.

A shouting interrupted them. Kiserian turned to see some warriors coming into the clearing.

"Go," the old woman said. "It is time for you to join your age mates in greeting the warriors. The wives will complete the meal."

Kiserian smiled her thanks and ran to the other girls already gathering outside of their hut. She stood by Kijeko, who was peering anxiously as more bands of warriors returned from the fighting.

"Your warrior will be among the brave," Kiserian said, trying to offer assurance.

"But I do not see him," Kijeko replied, "and those who were with him have returned."

"It is too soon to fear," Kiserian said. "He will come."

She heard a sharp breath from Kijeko and turned to see one of the leaders of the warriors walking toward their hut carrying two spears and two shields. Kiserian reached over, touched Kijeko's arm gently, and felt her friend tremble. The warrior stopped briefly, looking at the faces of the girls, and then moved on to another young woman down the row. Kijeko sighed.

The warrior faced the young woman solemnly. "It will be my duty to bring this shield and spear to his father." He took a bracelet off his wrist and handed it to her. With shaking hands, she took the bracelet and stared at it, expressionless. "Ngai has given this warrior to the hyenas, but you will hear the praises of his strength in battle around the fire tonight. *Gikuyu weep for their dead with only one eye.*"

The warrior turned abruptly and walked away.

***

The night was spent in celebration. There were no tears for the dead or pity for the wounded. Life and death belonged to Ngai alone.

Kijeko waited long into the evening for her warrior, but he did not return, and none knew of his whereabouts. A few days later, the warriors told her that she should join the dance again and find the feet of another. A true Gikuyu, Kijeko did not weep or speak of her loss. She rejoined the dance.

***

Kiserian danced with warriors for three seasons. She was a very popular dancing partner because she seemed to bring them good fortune in finding wives, but she did not step on the feet of a warrior more than once. Most of her age mates had found a warrior to marry; those who did not were destined to be second wives. It was becoming more common for elders young and old alike to step into the dance and put their hand on the shoulder of a young girl. This was usually arranged by their first wives, and the young girls were grateful to be second wives and to have no shame mentioned with their names. There were fewer warriors still looking at the remaining girls, and while they still danced with Kiserian, it was well understood that she was waiting for someone else.

At a dance not far from where her shushu lived, she saw Waitimu standing on the edge of the dancing circle. She smiled brightly at him, but he did not respond, and suddenly she feared that he had come to dance with someone else. Each dance she looked over to see if Waitimu had left the circle. Four warriors placed their hands on her shoulder, but she did not step on the feet of any that night.

Late in the evening, the women who had stepped on the feet of others broke away from the dance and led their suitors to the huts. Kiserian looked for Waitimu as she stepped in rhythm around the fire, but she did not see him. A feeling of panic set in.

She felt a hand gently touch her arm.

"Can you not find a warrior worthy of you tonight?"

"It is not a warrior that I wait for tonight," Kiserian said. She turned and pulled Waitimu deeper into the dancing circle. "There are plenty of younger women for the warriors."

"I have not danced as a warrior for a long time," he said. "You may find that my feet are no longer accustomed to the hard surface of the dancing circle, and that my hands know only to hold the digging stick in the shamba."

"When your feet grow tired of dancing, you need only to hold my shoulder like a digging stick and I will save you from any more dancing tonight."

Waitimu smiled. He hesitated for a moment before putting his hand on her shoulder. She stood quickly on his feet for a moment and then grabbed his hand and pulled him to the sleeping hut.

Inside, Waitimu gently stroked Kiserian's breasts. She felt shy but thrilled by his touch. He gently ran his hand down her stomach and legs. She felt him tremble, and she reached out and touched his chest. The warrior scars were long faded, but in their place were the sharply defined muscles of a farmer.

"I usually ask my warriors which clan they are from, so I can know if they would be acceptable as husbands for the clan of my mother."

Waitimu laughed softly. "And in three seasons you did not find a warrior that was acceptable for your clan?"

Kiserian smiled at him. "There have been none worthy enough to bother my mother."

"I know your mother well," Waitimu said. "I do not know what she might say about me."

"My mother would be pleased to hear of it if you chose me," Kiserian responded.

"There are not many mothers who would approve of me for their daughters," Waitimu said. "I had a first wife once, but she died without children. Most mothers would fear that I might have a curse and that it would be carried to their daughter."

"You mean, in the three seasons of my dancing, you have not yet found another first wife?"

"No, I am looking for a first wife, just like those warriors who dance with you every night," Waitimu said.

"We can dance every night until you decide," Kiserian said. "I would be your first wife, or your second wife if you want another first. But if you ask me, I will not look for another."

"I have danced enough," he said.

"I have danced for three full seasons," Kiserian said in mock surprise, "and you are tired already, when you have not completed even one dance?"

"I only danced to see if you would step on my feet. If you tell me you would step on my feet each time I touched your shoulder, it would save me from dancing with you again."

"My feet would always step on yours," she said.

"Then I will speak to my father about a bride-price and my mother about making honey for the honey beer."

"But who would get the bride-price?" Kiserian asked. She suddenly realized that she did not know what would happen next. "Does your father pay your mother, and then she gives it back to him?"

Waitimu laughed. His quest for a new wife seemed to be coming quickly to an end. "No, my father will contact the Maasai clan you came from through the N'dorobo man called Kihereko, who you met at the okijabe when you first came to live with us. He will be asked to find out if you have any living relatives. If the closest relative can be found, then sixty of my father's best sheep and goats will be sent to your Maasai relatives."

"Sixty! That is as much as a rich man would demand for one of his daughters."

"The Gikuyu do not negotiate with the Maasai unless they are also our relatives by blood. Since we cannot negotiate, it is our custom to pay the highest price, so that no one can say that we have bargained on our own behalf."

Kiserian thought about this for a long time, thrilled to hear that contact would be made with her Maasai relatives. She wondered how much she might learn from it. On the other hand, she was now a Gikuyu woman and no longer wanted to be a Maasai. Still, it would be satisfying to know that some of her relatives still lived.

"Tell me, then, how many more dances should I go to before I know what your intentions are?"

He laughed again. "You will never learn that a good Gikuyu does not ask questions so directly."

"I may never learn this lesson," Kiserian admitted with a smile. "You should consider that carefully."

"I have considered it since the day my mother brought you home from the Maasai," Waitimu said. "If you are tired of dancing, you should come back to your mother's shamba with me. If things go well with our mother, you can choose never to dance with warriors again."

"That has always been my choice," she said.

MANYATTA

Following the warrior's instructions, Ma'muriuki waited on the trail for the young Maasai boys to arrive with their cattle. When the boys appeared, the mother and her children followed behind silently. The young Maasai occasionally turned to watch the progress of the strangers, but they said nothing until they reached the opening of the enclosure. It seemed clear to the mother that the warriors had told the boys about her.

When they arrived at the manyatta, one of the boys turned and waited for Ma'muriuki while the others drove the cattle inside.

"My instructions are to tell the mother and her children to wait here outside the gate until the elders call for you to enter," the young boy said. He was speaking to the mother, but he was staring at Wangari.

"Thank you, my child," Ma'muriuki said. "We will wait here." She sat down and motioned for her girls to do the same.

The young boy turned to head into the enclosure and then stopped. He turned back and stared again at Wangari.

"Does the Maasai boy have more to say?" Ma'muriuki asked.

"Is it true that your daughters do not understand the words of the Maasai?"

"It is true, my child."

He hesitated and then came and sat down in front of Wangari. The Maasai boy and the Gikuyu girl quietly stared at each other.

The boy reached out and touched Wangari's face. He gently ran his fingers down her arms to her hands. He lifted her right hand and turned it over so that he could see the palm. He softly touched the large calluses on her hand and then looked at the mother. "I have heard that the Gikuyu women are like slaves to the men. Your daughter has very strong arms and the hands of one who has worked hard. But she is beautiful to see, and she does not look like a slave."

"My son, I was once a young girl among the Maasai. I too heard that Gikuyu women were slaves. But now I have lived among them. Gikuyu women work because they are proud and because they believe that Ngai requires hard work. Gikuyu women are slaves to no one. My daughter who sits before you has heard that Maasai are mighty warriors but lazy thieves. But the Maasai and the Gikuyu do not understand the ways of others. My daughter will soon learn what it means to live among the Maasai. She will learn that not everything she has heard about the Maasai is true."

Wangari took her hand away from the young boy and began to touch his face and arms. She took his hand and turned it over. "Mama, these hands have never worked in a shamba. He is strong, but he does not know work."

"Does the young Gikuyu girl know how to take milk from a cow? And does she know how to check for disease?" the Maasai boy asked.

"Yes," Ma'muriuki said.

"Good," the boy replied. "She will do well among the Maasai women." His smile showed bright white teeth. "I will return." He ran into the enclosure.

"What did the Maasai boy want, Mama?"

Before Ma'muriuki had finished explaining their

conversation, the boy reappeared, leading a cow out of the manyatta. He stopped just in front of Wangari, untied a gourd hanging from his side, and handed it to the young girl. "My mother said that it would be good for the strangers to have milk while they wait for the elders." He took a step back and watched Wangari.

The young girl flashed a smile at the boy. She walked around the cow, examining its hooves, eyes, and teeth. "This is a healthy cow, Mama, but it is not as fat as our cattle."

"My daughter says that you brought a healthy cow," Ma'muriuki said.

The boy's teeth flashed white again. "Our cattle are the best in the world, because all cattle belong to the Maasai."

The mother turned to Wangari. "The young Maasai boy thanks you for your kind words about the cattle that belong to his manyatta."

Wangari grinned at the boy. She moved closer and began to milk the cow, carefully getting all the contents into the narrow-necked gourd.

"I will take the gourd to my mother to prepare it for you," the boy said.

"You are very kind, my son, but my daughters do not yet know the way the Maasai prepare the milk. Would your mother be offended if my daughters drink the milk without the Maasai preparation?"

The boy paused in indecision. "I will ask my mother."

He disappeared again into the manyatta. This time it took longer for him to reappear. When he did, he handed the gourd to Ma'muriuki. "My mother did not understand at first, but others helped her to understand."

"Tell your mother, I am grateful for her understanding," Ma'muriuki said.

"What did that boy do with the milk, Mama?"

"His mother blessed the milk."

"He does not look like a lazy thief, Mama, and he respects his mother," Wangari said.

"Yes, my child. The world is not as you think."

Once the milk was passed around, Wangari stood up and handed the gourd back to the Maasai boy. "How do I say 'thank you,' Mama?" she asked, looking back to her mother.

"You say *ashe*, my child, and then touch your heart with your hand."

"*Ashe*," Wangari said. She touched her heart.

The young boy laughed in delight and clapped his hands. "What words would I say in return?" he asked.

"*Nĩndamũnyita ũgeni*," Ma'muriuki told him.

The boy struggled to repeat the Gikuyu phrase. Wangari giggled at his failed attempt.

"I think you now have a Maasai friend," Ma'muriuki said to her.

The boy pointed to the cow and gave the Maasai word for it. Wangari grinned and responded in Gikuyu. Soon the two were picking up sticks, rocks, and clothing, telling each other what the objects were in their language.

"I see the Maasai woman with Gikuyu children has found the child who cannot stop talking."

Startled, Ma'muriuki looked up to see the warrior who had given her directions to the manyatta earlier in the day.

"I see the moran sent word ahead that we were coming. I am grateful," she said.

"It may be that this moran has decided to plant his spear outside of your enkaji tonight."

"The warrior would be welcome. But surely there are other wives in the manyatta who would be willing to spread their legs for a moran like you," Ma'muriuki said.

"Yes, many," the warrior said. His eyes showed amusement. "But those women will be here tomorrow night as well. It may be that other warriors might not understand why the Maasai woman with Gikuyu children does not spread her legs. It would be better if I stayed with you tonight."

"You are welcome. I will have many questions."

"And I have questions as well. Our world has changed forever. I hear that the Gikuyu world has also changed. It is hard to accept what I have heard."

"Yes," Ma'muriuki said, "the world has changed forever."

"Now, let me go inside and find out what is taking those old men so long to talk about you." He turned and walked into the manyatta, motioning for the young boy to follow him.

***

Ma'muriuki heard the telltale scraping sound and thud of a spear being stabbed into the ground outside of the enkaji. The girls were startled at the sound and looked at their mother. She smiled at them and waited for the Maasai moran to speak.

"Maasai woman with Gikuyu children, I have planted my spear outside the door of your enkaji." The warrior's voice carried loud, and Ma'muriuki understood that he wanted others to hear his announcement.

Her voice matched his. "The warrior is welcome."

The warrior stooped as he stepped into the enkaji. He briefly greeted Ma'muriuki and then turned his attention to the children, touching the girls' hair and arms. He took their hands and put them on his own arms, and soon Wangari and Makena were exploring his face and long plaited hair. When they touched the broadsword at his side, he smiled, removed it from its sheath, and handed it to them to examine. Without a single word, the warrior and the girls grew comfortable with each other.

He moved on to little Maathai, patting the boy on the head and reaching out for him.

Ma'muriuki hesitated, and then handed her young son to him.

"So, you have named this one Maathai. It seems you have not forgotten that you were once a Maasai woman," he said. "I have a son this age, but he lives with my wife in another manyatta."

"I can see you are a good father."

"Yes," the warrior said.

Maathai started to cry. The warrior bounced the boy on his knee and the cries turned to giggles. Soon the boy was asleep in his arms.

He spoke quietly to Ma'muriuki. "The elders discussed your case and have asked me to tell you what they have decided."

"Speak," she said.

"It will be difficult for you to find the manyatta where your brothers live if you travel alone with your children. The elders agreed to have the young boy who spoke with you outside the fence take you there. It is a three-day journey to your brothers' manyatta. If you agree, the boy will go with you in two days, after you and your children have rested. For now, you can stay in this enkaji."

"I am grateful to the warrior for his help. I will accept the elders' advice. My daughter will be glad that the young boy will be traveling with us."

"Good." He settled back, leaning against the wall of the house. "Now tell me about the Gikuyu. I have a sister who lives among those people."

"Ah!" the mother said. "Now I better understand your kindness. There is much to tell."

UNDER THE MUGUMO TREE

Waitimu and Kiserian stood quietly as they gazed at Shushu Njoki, her body wrapped in a goatskin and her sleeping mat, tightly bound by the flexible roots of the *muoha* plant. Only her face remained uncovered.

"Ngai alone decides when it is time for his children to return to him," Waitimu said to his wife. "It is time for our mother to rejoin her husband among the ancestors. We weep with only one eye because we know that we too will join our ancestors beneath the roots of the mugumo tree when it is our time."

Kiserian nodded and smiled resolutely. It was long past time for her shushu to be with the ancestors, but for her, the old woman was the essence of everything she had learned about her people.

It had only been one season earlier when Kiserian watched Waitimu build the temporary shelter for his ailing father, next to the burial ground just beyond the fence. The Gikuyu homestead belonged to the wife, not the husband, so when a man appeared to be dying, he was placed in a temporary shelter until he died or recovered enough to return to his home. Waitimu sat day and night outside the hut, watching his father and waiting to see if he would live or die. When the old man finally left the earth and made his journey to join the ancestors beneath the mugumo tree, Waitimu burned the temporary hut and planted *muoha* plants to mark the spot so that no one would build a hut or plant there again.

When Shushu Njoki was near death, she was not removed from her hut like her husband, as it was fitting that she spend her last hours in the home that belonged to her.

Kiserian sat in her Gikuyu mother's hut and watched the old woman fade quietly into death with the same dignity she had demonstrated in life. As word spread of her having joined the ancestors, relatives began to gather. She was a great woman, and no one wanted to be haunted by her spirit for not showing respect.

It was Waitimu's duty, as the only remaining son, to bury his mother. He paid five goats to a relative to help him perform the rituals. As he had no father to give him instructions, he paid an elder another five goats to instruct him on how to perform the necessary tasks.

Kiserian did not touch the body once she realized that her shushu was no longer living; to do so would have made her unclean in the community until she offered a goat in sacrifice to Ngai. She was only allowed to sit and watch her husband carry out the burial duties. She wanted to do something to show honor, but honor for a daughter is silence.

Even Waitimu and his helper were very careful not to touch the dead woman during the preparation process. They used sticks and vines to lift and wrap the body, and they placed wooden poles underneath to carry it to the burial site. Later, they would sacrifice a goat to Ngai just in case they had mistakenly touched the body unawares.

They carried the shushu's bundled body to the appointed burial spot, in the bushes behind the house. There they cut two long branches from a young *mubiru* tree and sharpened them to use as digging stakes. The stakes used for burial were always new and buried with the body. While the two men dug the hole, the elder surveyed the crowd of onlookers to make certain that all living relatives were present. A missing relative could delay the burial for as many as eight days, after which time they risked a certain curse from the deceased spirit. But all were present, and the elder lit a fire next to the grave so that the smoke would carry any unwanted spirits away from the site.

Waitimu and his helper lowered the body into the hole so it lay on its left side facing the house. Then they covered the body quickly with soil.

When Waitimu rejoined his young wife, he warned, "Be careful not to touch me until my hair has been shaved and the goat has been sacrificed, or you will become unclean."

Kiserian nodded absently, her mind on the day her shushu had shouted to her husband to prepare honey beer, for her son and daughter were to be married. It was a happy day, followed by many more.

***

When Shushu Njoki first saw her son Waitimu and her Maasai daughter returning from the dance festivals, she shouted to her husband, "I think it is time for me to press the sugar cane so you can make beer. We have many days of celebration before us."

The elders were soon called. As expected, it was agreed by all that even though both Kiserian and Waitimu had the same mother and were from the same clan, the fact that Kiserian was first born a Maasai was sufficient reason to ignore any restrictions on their marriage. But the elders insisted that the protocol of the marriage proposal and the marriage itself be followed. One elder was chosen to act on behalf of Kiserian's Maasai family, and she was moved temporarily into the home of the elder's first wife.

Waitimu walked to his father's hut, where he called out for and received permission to enter. Inside, they sat on stools facing each other, both smiling, though the old man pretended he did not know the purpose of his son's visit.

"Why has my son come to disturb me in my house? Is this the time of day for talking, or should my son be working in the shamba?"

"My father, I have found a shamba that belongs to another man, and I want to farm it."

"No man owns a shamba, my son. All shambas belong to Ngai. We are only blessed to be given use of lands that belong to Ngai to bring crops as we have been commanded."

"Yes, father, but nevertheless, there is land that Ngai has given to another, upon which I wish to plant a garden."

"Do you know what clan this man is from?"

"Yes, father, the clan is one that the elders have allowed us to negotiate with."

"Then, my son, have you talked to the mother of the house?"

"Yes, father, I went there yesterday."

"Tell me, what happened at the house of the mother?"

"I went to the house with three of my friends. We sat and visited with the mother and her daughter. The mother asked me the purpose of my visit, and I told her that I wished to farm in her shamba. She then left us alone with her daughter. My friend told the daughter that we wanted her to marry us. She said that she cannot marry four men. But my friend insisted she must choose to marry one of us, or she must choose to marry none of us.

"When the mother came back, she carried four gourds of gruel for us to drink. She handed the gruel to the daughter, who gave gourds to my three friends. But before she gave me my gourd to drink, she took a sip of the gruel first and then handed it to me."

The old man leaned back and tried to act surprised. "Then this girl has told you that she is willing to marry you, and her mother would not have brought the gruel if her husband refused you for a son."

Waitimu smiled. "I have been told that the father of this girl is a cruel man, and that he does not take kindly to men asking to marry his daughter. I am deeply honored that he has approved."

By this time, both men were trying hard to contain their laughter. "Careful, my son, do not mock an old father, for there is still time for him to change his mind about this marriage. But for now, we will ask that old woman I married to bring me some more honey beer." He shouted for his wife through the walls of the hut.

In her enkaji, Shushu Njoki picked up a large pot of honey beer to take to her husband.

"Shushu," Kiserian asked, "why do the elders want us to go through this engagement ceremony when it is already agreed that we can marry?"

"My daughter, do you not yet understand the ways of the Gikuyu? In the engagement ceremonies, you will have four opportunities to turn down the marriage offer by Waitimu. It is not our way to force someone to do what they do not want to do. The elders want you to go through the full ceremony so that everyone will know this marriage is something you want and not something that I or my son is forcing you to do."

"I understand, Shushu," Kiserian said.

The old woman smiled at her daughter and carried the honey beer to her husband's hut.

***

One month after Shushu Njoki died, Kiserian went to the shamba to work in the field. Waitimu was not out cutting trees and breaking new ground as usual. At first she thought he might have gone to a meeting with the elders. It was time for him to bring them a sheep to begin the process of becoming an elder himself. Every day, they hoped that she would become pregnant. Then, soon after the birth, it would be time for him to take his second sheep to the elders and be accepted as a first-level elder.

She felt her stomach, but there were no signs of a child. She wanted a child. She wanted to be the giver of life for Ngai and to bring honor to her husband. She smiled in anticipation. Her pregnancy would end any idea from the clan that her husband might still be cursed from his first wife's death.

Then Kiserian noticed a dark form on the edge of the

forest, an unusual shape on the ground. As she walked toward it, she recognized the clothing and the shaved head and she ran. But it was not until she saw the swarm of flies over the figure that she screamed.

MAASAI WOMEN

Ma'muriuki sat looking at her older brother. Like her father long ago, her brother was a respected elder, leader, and spiritual man among the Maasai. He was clearly in complete control of the manyatta. His face triggered distant memories of her father.

Her other brother sat with the council of men at the entrance to the manyatta. Her brothers had told her earlier that there were no other family members alive. Her mother's sons had died before she left the Maasai. These brothers, she decided, must have belonged to one of her father's other wives.

"Will we be asked by the stupid Gikuyu"—her brother paused to spit on the ground—"to return the marriage sheep and goats to them?"

"No, they will not ask. I have broken no custom, and I have not dishonored my marriage. The Gikuyu know that the Maasai do not give their livestock away to others."

From where she sat, the Gikuyu lands were little more than a distant blue line on the horizon.

"Good. So, my sister, what are you, then? Are you still a Maasai, or have you become a Gikuyu like your children?"

"My brother, I am here among the Maasai, and I still speak

the language of Enkai. When my mother sent me to live among the Gikuyu, they waited for me to decide if I would remain a Maasai, or if I would become a Gikuyu. I am now among the Maasai. Will my own brothers give me the same chance to decide who I am, as the Gikuyu did, or do you wish to make me your Gikuyu slave?"

"You will wait for our answer," her brother said. "For now, you will stay in this enkaji until the council has made a decision." He pointed to the empty hut behind her and then got up and joined his brother and the council of men. A lengthy conversation ensued.

Ma'muriuki saw that as the men talked, they turned from time to time to look at her and her children. She had felt certain that once she found relatives, especially brothers, no harm would come to her. No Maasai would risk insulting Enkai by abusing a woman who might belong to the Maasai.

Deciding not to wait any longer for them to make their decision, she stepped inside the empty enkaji that would be her temporary home. It looked as if it had been empty for several months. The floor was muddy from last night's rain. Certainly, the walls and leaking roof were in poor shape. She reached up, pushed on the roof, and was satisfied that at least the construction was still strong.

Ma'muriuki stepped outside again and realized that her girls were quietly following her every step. They had not said a word since they arrived at the manyatta. "My children, we do not know how long we will live here, so today we will begin to do the work of Maasai women. If we do our work well, perhaps it will make it easier to stay with these people."

Wangari and Makena nodded.

"Follow me," their mother said, motioning to her girls.

The other women, on their roofs repairing the damage from the previous night's downpour, stopped and looked at her. Ma'muriuki still had Maathai wrapped on her back, Gikuyu style. It would be better in the eyes of the other women to put the child on the ground to fend for himself like the other small children, but she was not yet ready to leave him on his own in such an unfamiliar place. She led her girls to the area where the goats, sheep, and cattle milled quietly inside the manyatta enclosure.

"Watch me, children, and then you will do what I am doing." She scooped up a fresh pile of manure and mixed it with the sandy soil. "Now feel this." She handed portions of the mixture to each of her daughters. "Not too wet, not too dry," she said, hoping that she remembered how to repair a roof. "This is called *aitushul*. Now mix as much as you can carry and follow me."

Wangari immediately caught on and made a sizable pile of aitushul. Makena seemed confused, so her sister helped her make a small mixture for herself. They carried their piles in their hands under the silent, watchful gaze of the Maasai women perched on their roofs. Ma'muriuki lifted her girls onto the roof of her enkaji and placed the piles beside them. She boosted herself up from a small ledge on the wall.

"Now watch me, children." The mother worked the manure mix into the cracks in the roof. She paused to observe Wangari's efforts. "Good, child. You keep working on the roof, and Makena and I will keep you supplied with the aitushul." She hopped down and led her younger daughter back to the animals.

The manyatta women chattered to each other. Ma'muriuki tried to ignore them, but it was clear the women were impressed that she understood how to fix a roof. It was also clear the women thought that her roof was beyond repair. She smiled at this.

The Maasai men also noticed her efforts while they talked, a few of them pointing to Ma'muriuki and the girls. From the corner of her eye, she watched the other women hop off their roofs one at a time as they finished their work. They were not dressed as she remembered Maasai women dressing. They wore strange-looking bands of necklaces around their necks. The colors of the beads were bright and colorful. Ma'muriuki could not think of any seeds or berries in the Maasai world with such color. What the necklaces were made of was a mystery to her, as well as what purpose they served the women.

Refocusing on her roof, she climbed up again and sent Wangari down to help Makena. After watching her daughters run back to collect more manure and sand, she looked at the work that Wangari had done; it was not perfect, but she was very proud of her daughter's first attempts.

She cleaned up Wangari's work as she waited for her girls to return. Hearing the soft thud of more mixture dropping onto the roof behind her, she turned to thank her daughters but was startled by the sight of one of the Maasai women on the roof instead.

"Your daughters work very hard," the woman said, "but if you are to be done by nightfall, you will need our help."

"I am grateful," Ma'muriuki said. "I have not worked on an enkaji since I was a young girl, and this is the first time for my daughters."

"You speak the language of Enkai very well," another woman said as she too placed a pile of aitushul on the roof. "Your mixture is too dry to work with; you will find ours to be better for a roof as bad as this one."

Ma'muriuki's girls arrived, carrying their piles. One of the women helped them put the mixture on the roof and then motioned for them to follow her. "Tell your daughters that I will teach them to mix the aitushul with grass to make your repairs stronger," the woman said.

Two other women joined her on the roof patching holes while a parade of women brought more aitushul to them in a steady rhythm. Ma'muriuki looked around for her girls.

"Your daughters have finished mixing the aitushul and are now with my daughter, looking after the newborn goats," a woman said.

Ma'muriuki gave the woman a smile of appreciation. "My children know nothing of this world. I am grateful for the kindness of the women here. My world has changed, and nothing is as it used to be. I do not know what the world will be for my children."

"The world has changed for all of us," the woman replied.

"I do not know what my brothers and the council will decide, but I hope we can stay in this manyatta, and I hope I can help my children learn the words of Enkai and the ways of the Maasai."

"Your brother plants his spear outside my door often," the woman said. She smiled at Ma'muriuki. "If they make a bad decision, I will let his spear rust in the dirt."

Several of the women laughed. "His spear has tasted the dirt at all of our doors," another woman said. "My husband says that he gives us good children."

"Your brothers are good elders," a third woman said. "They have built our cattle into a healthy herd, and our manyatta is respected by all the morani. Your father was a great man among our people, and we are honored to have another of his children among us."

"You are a desirable woman in the eyes of men. Even my husband told me that he is ready to plant his spear at your door when the time is right," the first woman said.

Ma'muriuki felt a slight revulsion but hoped her face did not show it. "I was a child when I left the Maasai," she said. "I remember that morani who were loyal to my father would plant their spears outside of my mother's enkaji. I also know that a woman who welcomes a man who has planted a spear is not required to take his seed. But I do not know what one says to let a man know that she is willing to spread her legs for him."

"There is plenty of time before a man will plant his spear at your door looking to plant his seed," the woman said. "We will teach you these things before that time comes. It would be better to establish yourself with a husband before spreading your legs when a spear is planted at your door. I think that any man in this manyatta would be glad to make you his wife, except your brothers."

All the women laughed.

Ma'muriuki smiled. "I am not yet free to take a Maasai man to be my husband," she said. "I have a son, Muriuki, who is still among the Gikuyu, and I cannot sever my ties with them and lose my son. I do not know if I am able to be both a Gikuyu and a Maasai. Until I know, I do not think I can spread my legs for a man."

"Is this son the reason you are called Ma'muriuki?"

"Yes, the mother is given a name of honor from her first born. When I lived among the Gikuyu, I kept my Maasai name, Kiserian. But when my first child, Muriuki, was born, I was given the honored title of Mama Muriuki. The Gikuyu shorten the title to Ma'muriuki, and that is now my name. My husband was a good man, but now he rests among the ancestors."

"Why have you come among us, then? Do those stupid Gikuyu not provide for their own?"

"They do," Ma'muriuki said. "But the world has changed for the Gikuyu."

"The world has changed for all of us," the woman said.

An older woman motioned for silence and the others fell quiet. "It is best that the daughter of the great Naengop listen to my words," she said in a soft voice. "You have a great advantage because you are the sister of great men and the daughter of a greater man. No harm will come to you any time soon because of these things. But there will come a time when you must decide if you are a Maasai or a Gikuyu. The legs of a Maasai woman are spread only by the consent of the Maasai woman. But morani are not concerned about the consent of a Gikuyu woman. You must weigh carefully these things. Right now there is a period of peace between our clan and the Gikuyu, but the peace between the Gikuyu and the Maasai does not last more than one season or two before we steal cattle and goats from each other again. You should not think that you can stay between these two worlds for very long."

Ma'muriuki was quiet for a while. She began to speak and then stopped. The woman waited for her. Finally, she said, "You speak wise words, my mother, and I listen with understanding. What you have said is my chief concern. I know I cannot be long among the Maasai unless I choose to be a Maasai. I also know I cannot choose to drive a world between my son and myself. I do not know what to do, but I am eager to hear your counsel on this matter."

The woman put her hand over her heart to indicate respect for Ma'muriuki. "My child, the women here understand your dilemma, and we will protect you as long as we can. Some of the women here receive visions from the spirits of our ancestors at night. It is possible that one of them will hear from an ancestor and give you counsel. We will not force you to be one of us, but choose wisely, because things will not go well for you if there is no one to protect you here. But until that time comes, we welcome you among us, and we will teach you the ways that you have forgotten."

The women returned to working on the roof of the enkaji, stopping often for conversation and laughter. In Ma'muriuki's Gikuyu world, they would not have stopped until the job was completed, but the Maasai women seemed less interested in the work than in conversation.

The sun was beginning to cast long shadows when the, the council of men broke up and Ma'muriuki's brother came over to her.

"I see the women of the manyatta have made their decision about our guest before the men have finished their council," the brother said.

"I hope the council of men chose wisely," a woman said matter-of-factly.

He smiled. "We do not want our spears to become rusty outside the doors of angry women." He turned to Ma'muriuki. "You are welcome here, but the men want you to choose before this season comes again. For now, you can stay in the enkaji you are repairing. If you choose a Maasai man, then you can build your own enkaji." He began to leave and then stopped and faced her again. "It is good to see another of my father's children. I am glad you have come." He turned abruptly and walked away.

"The council chose wisely," a woman said. "You are

welcome among us."

***

The next morning, Ma'muriuki woke up with a start. The sun was already up. She stepped out the door quickly and then remembered she did not have a shamba to work in that day. She was surprised that no one was outside of their houses except for a few morani guarding the entrances and some boys preparing to lead the livestock out to pasture. Thoughts of Maasai laziness overwhelmed her. By that hour, all of the Gikuyu women would be working in the shambas and the men would be in council or breaking up new ground for their wives to plant produce.

She climbed up onto the roof to catch the morning breezes and watch the manyatta slowly wake up. She tried to remember being a young girl in a manyatta, but it seemed more like a dream than a memory.

The women soon emerged from their huts and sat in a circle. They waved her down from the roof to join them. Ma'muriuki climbed down and poked her head into her new little home. All three of her children were quietly waiting for her. "My children, come out from this dark place and enjoy the light of the day."

"Mama, we do not know what our duties are," Wangari said.

Ma'muriuki wondered if she had made a mistake coming to the Maasai lands. Would her children stop learning how to work and bring produce from the ground? Would they become lazy Maasai women, talking incessantly about their lovers? She had a feeling there was little she could do to change things.

"My children, there are no duties today." She left them to contemplate the possibility of nothing to do and joined the women in the circle. They were busily threading thin strings made from braided roots through holes in the colorful round beads she had seen them wear the day before.

Ma'muriuki picked up one of the beads and looked at it closely. "I do not understand these things," she said. "I do

146

not remember these objects from my childhood."

"We trade for these with the Red People," one of the women said. "Now we use them to make decorations for our necks."

"I do not understand what you mean by the 'Red People,'" Ma'muriuki said.

"The Gikuyu call them the Butterfly People," the woman replied. "When you were young, we lost many of our people and cattle to disease when the angry face of Nanyoki was against us. After that, our great leader died and a war broke out between his two sons as they struggled to become the new head elder of the Maasai people. A son named Lenana won the right to be the head elder, but the fighting continued. That is when the Red People came. They were too powerful for us because we were too weak from disease and war. Our head elder, Lenana, negotiated peace with them, and in return they allowed him to be both the head elder and the chief of our people."

"I do not understand the word 'chief,'" Ma'muriuki said.

"The Red People insist that every people must have leaders called 'chiefs' to rule the others. They make judgments on some issues and give other judgments to the Red People to settle."

"Why do the Maasai need chiefs? Don't they have elders to make judgments for them?"

"The Red People were too powerful for us to fight with them about their ways. We were too few to resist. They have taken lands that we once used when we had many cattle, and they restrict our passage in those lands. They tell us that we are to obey their laws. They trade with us, and that is how we get these colorful beads."

Ma'muriuki felt a knot in her stomach. She quickly put the little bead down. "Why are they called the Red People?"

"They hide from the world with many skins, but their faces turn red when they see the sun."

"Our world has changed," Ma'muriuki said. The women nodded their agreement again.

She thought about Muriuki and the words of the medicine man. He had predicted that she would be kept safe in her journey to the Maasai. She wondered if she dared to hope that his words about her seeing Muriuki again might also come true. Ngai had kept her safe; perhaps Ngai would still bless her and her children through Muriuki.

AHOI

Kiserian spent her days working alone in the shamba where, only a few months before, she had been working behind Waitimu. At night she spent sleepless hours staring into the darkness until light began to filter through the walls. Each day was the same. Working, staring at darkness, and working again. She was waiting.

Her case as a young widow without children quickly became a topic of discussion among the clan elders. Waitimu had inherited considerable land and cattle from his parents, not to mention his own accumulation of assets. Without a son, there was no male child to take the inheritance. Eventually, the land would filter back to other relatives, but as long as Kiserian was young and still in her childbearing years, her male offspring would be the first to inherit. It was important to the community to keep the land within the clan and, if at all possible, within the same family.

Gichina was the closest relative to Waitimu that was eligible for marriage. According to tradition, he was the first choice to take responsibility for Kiserian and to give her children who would inherit Waitimu's land. As far as the elders knew, Gichina was not a bad man, but by Gikuyu standards, he was a lazy man. The elders' concern about

149

Gichina's character led them to debate Kiserian's case for a long time. She had a good reputation as a strong Gikuyu woman who had been taught well by her shushu, and she was a mate fit for a much more worthy man. Gichina was more like the hyena who cared only to fill his belly. But tradition was strong in such cases, and the elders finally decided that there was no choice other than to offer Gichina to Kiserian as a surrogate husband. As the Gikuyu saying went, *It is not often that a good mortar finds a good pestle.*

By then it had become clear to all that Waitimu and his family had been cursed by the clan of his first wife. No one knew if this curse had carried to Kiserian. A more suitable husband might be reluctant to take the chance.

At last the council assigned one of their elders to speak on their behalf to Kiserian. It was clear from his choice of words that the council was not in favor of Gichina as a mate for her.

"My child," the old man began, "no elder expects you to accept this Gichina as the one to give you children to inherit the lands that Ngai gave Waitimu. If you choose not to accept this arrangement, the council will find the next relative for you. This Gichina will not change. *There is no mother once one has become a man.*"

"You are kind," Kiserian said, "but it will be difficult for me to find a relative who does not fear there may be a curse on me from my husband's first wife. It is my obligation to Ngai to have children to take the inheritance from Waitimu."

"You are young, my child," he said. "You are strong and still a beautiful woman. There are still good men who need wives."

"I am grateful for your concern," she replied. "But I do not know how many seasons may pass until such a good man is found. My obligation to Ngai is not for myself, but for those who will inherit my husband's land. I will accept Gichina. I will work hard in his shamba, and I will bear children to inherit the lands that belong to Waitimu."

It was settled. With the elders' supervision, Kiserian

leased all of Waitimu's livestock to poorer clanspeople and all of the cultivated portions of Waitimu's land to ahoi. The uncultivated parts would remain fallow until she had produced an inheritor to work them.

Kiserian moved into the newly constructed first wife's hut next to Gichina's hut. Early in the morning the day after she moved in, she went to Gichina's small field and began to cultivate it. That same evening, she carried a gourd of bitter gruel with his evening meal to let him know she was ready for a conjugal visit.

***

For Gichina, Kiserian's decision was a gift beyond his imagination. His status was poor in the community. He should have already found a wife, even a poor or ugly one, to work on his inherited lands. But he had only cultivated a small section of them, and the rest he had allowed to return to the forests. He did not have enough livestock to pay a full dowry, nor was there a potential father-in-law willing to risk a man of Gichina's reputation working off the debt of a bride-price. *Cows are not obtained by lazy people.*

For most men, securing a bride-price would not have been a problem. If their parents could not afford the price, they would have either gone on a raid to the Maasai lands to retrieve some of their stolen livestock, or they would have worked as an ahoi on the land of the future father-in-law until enough animals were obtained to begin dowry payments. But Gichina blamed the world for his misfortunes and did not work to overcome them. *The lazy one blames the instruments.*

Kiserian was not technically his wife. Gichina was a surrogate for her deceased husband; she and her future children still belonged to Waitimu. But she was a beautiful and hardworking Gikuyu woman who would make full use of the little shamba that Gichina had cleared, and, most importantly, she would give him some status in the community. Perhaps he could find a way to use the wealth of her unborn children's property to pay for a first wife of his own.

***

When Kiserian gave birth to her first child, there was great excitement in the community. The midwife and her helpers gave five ululations when they determined that it was a boy. When the relatives outside heard that she had given birth to a son, they congratulated each other between sips of honey beer.

"It is a good thing that the owner of Waitimu's lands has come to this house," they said to one another.

No one paid attention to Gichina, who sat quietly, drinking beer out of his cow horn cup. The day Kiserian's first child was born was the day he began to despise her. Her children would be the glory of Waitimu. No one praised Gichina.

After the eighth day, Kiserian emerged from the house with a healthy boy. For the first eight days after birth, the child was given no name because he was still a part of the mother. On the ninth day, the child belonged to Ngai.

Kiserian announced that the boy's name would be Muriuki, the name of Waitimu's father. "It is fitting that my son be named Muriuki," she said, "because my husband's inheritance has now been reborn in my son."

"This is as it should be," her relatives said to each other. "She is a mother now; her name is no longer Kiserian, but Mama Muriuki. She will be called Ma'muriuki."

Gichina had expected the son to be named after his own father, and so he despised Ma'muriuki even more.

When Wangari was born, three seasons later, there were four ululations for a girl, and Ma'muriuki named her after her shushu's mother. By this time, even the relatives noticed that Gichina was becoming increasingly hostile toward Ma'muriuki. His accusations that she did not do enough work in the shamba were not true, and everyone knew it. He was drinking more honey beer, and no one saw him breaking new ground in the shamba anymore.

***

One evening, Ma'muriuki brought Gichina a portion of

boiled yams and bananas for his evening meal. "I think it is time for me to find a first wife for my husband," she said. She then set a gourd of bitter gruel next to the food.

"This is too cold," he said. He picked up the gruel and hardly glanced at the food.

"I will find you a wife to give you children to inherit your land," she said. She ignored his comment about the meal because they both knew the food was perfect. She hoped a wife of his own would make him feel more important, and then he would not be so harsh with her. Even her age mates warned her that one day his anger might turn to violence.

"You know I do not have the livestock to pay a bride-price." He glared at her in disgust. "You spend your days taking care of Waitimu's inheritance and do not provide enough in the field for me to purchase livestock. You have brought your husband's curse to my house."

Ma'muriuki kept the tiny arable portion of the shamba fully productive. She had even cleared more land—when he was not around so as not to shame him—in order to plant more produce, for *the lazy one eats only what others have harvested.* But he did notice that she had done his work for him and despised her even more for it.

"I will pay the bride-price for my husband's first wife from the inheritance of my children," she said.

Gichina spat angrily on the ground and motioned for her to leave his hut. It was her fault that he was not getting ahead. It was her fault that he had not gained status with the marriage. It was her responsibility to resolve this by getting him another wife. And it had taken her too long to finally realize this.

***

There were rumors that the Butterfly People had moved into the lands of Gikuyu clans on distant ridges. However, Ma'muriuki was too busy working in the shamba and looking for a new wife for Gichina to be bothered with wild stories about the powers and magic of these strange people.

Her search for a wife for Gichina was rewarded when she

found Ngeri. Ngeri was an age mate of Ma'muriuki, but her first husband died in battle before she, too, could have children. Ngeri was grateful to Ma'muriuki for giving her a home, and the two worked well together in the shamba. Ngeri took over the first wife's house, and a second wife's house was built for Ma'muriuki.

That was when ahoi from other clans began to show up. They all had once been landowners in good standing, but the Butterfly People took their lands. The strangers had given them a choice: stay on their own lands as ahoi to the Butterfly People or leave and not return. The Butterfly People were too powerful to resist.

It was rumored by some that the Butterfly People hired Maasai warriors to protect them from the Gikuyu whose lands they had taken. At first, no one in Ma'muriuki's clan believed that the Maasai would do such a thing. After all, the Gikuyu and the Maasai squabbled and sometimes fought over livestock, but they were all children of the same father.

Initially, just a few ahoi appeared, and the clan was able to accept them. Then the number of ahoi increased so rapidly that the clan was overwhelmed. The newcomers began squatting on uncultivated portions of clan lands. Soon they were living on Ma'muriuki's lands.

Like all wealthy landowners, Ma'muriuki was willing to lease the uncultivated portions of her children's inheritance to the ahoi until they could purchase land of their own.

Gichina had other ideas. He sold some of her children's land to the ahoi in exchange for future livestock. The rest of the inherited land he sold to other relatives. As respected as Ma'muriuki was in the community, she could not defend her children's inheritance. The elders were too busy settling the lawsuits against the ahoi brought to them by the living to be bothered with a case on behalf of one who was already with the ancestors. Ma'muriuki watched helplessly as Waitimu's inheritance slipped away.

Her world had changed forever.

THE RIVER

Gichina was an angry man when he was sober and a violent man when he was drunk. He quickly squandered the proceeds from the land he stole from Ma'muriuki's children. He blamed all his misfortunes on Ma'muriuki, which was why he beat her so badly. He beat his Ngeri as well, but not as often as Ma'muriuki.

"The world has changed," Ngeri told Ma'muriuki. "It was not long ago when a man was fined many goats for beating his wives, but now no one can be bothered."

She was sitting in Ma'muriuki's house, washing out the new wounds in her co-wife's back with water. She pressed a mixture of *ngwaci ya ngoma* flowers and the bark of the *mutamaiyu* tree against the broken skin and saw that one wound was deep. Ngeri carefully inserted three long *muthuthi* bush thorns through both sides of the cut. She then laced the broken edges of the skin together by wrapping a thin string of leather around each end of the thorns.

Ma'muriuki sat still throughout the procedure and showed no indication of pain as her co-wife took care of her injuries.

"We are still Gikuyu women," she said, "and Ngai is still among us. We still have elders who sit on the council. Is there no opportunity for our voices to be heard?"

155

"For me, there is an opportunity," Ngeri said. "I can return to my father's house, and if my family hears my complaint, he will go to the elders to end the marriage and demand compensation for me and my child." She patted her bulging stomach to emphasize her new status as an expecting mother. "But for you, I do not know. You have no Gikuyu family still walking on this earth to call our husband to judgment. You can call upon the ancestors, but this man does not fear their curses. You have no family now, except for those who may be scattered among the Maasai."

"This is why he beats me so harshly," Ma'muriuki said. "He does not believe that there are those who will defend me or protect my children. The world has changed, but I still believe that Ngai and the ancestors will hear me."

She had given birth to both Makena and Maathai before Ngeri became pregnant, but once Gichina heard that Ngeri was with child, his beatings of Ma'muriuki became vicious.

"Oh, my friend," Ngeri said, "I thought our husband would stop hitting you when he learned that I will have his child." She motioned that she was finished cleaning up the wounds. "Now I know he will not stop. One day you will be carried out from this hut to be buried by your relatives."

"*The beginning of a matter is not as regretted as the end,*" Ma'muriuki said. "I thought at first he would release his anger toward me when he took you as a wife. When that did not stop him, I then hoped he would no longer beat me when he learned he had his own child. Gichina has no more use for me, now that he has stolen my children's inheritance. I know he will not stop beating me. He has no respect for Ngai or the ways of the Gikuyu. He beats you too, my friend. *A rat ruins a hide by its constant gnawing.*"

"Yes, but my wounds are not deep, and if he continues, my relatives will take me back and sue him for the damages. But where will you go? You have no relatives among the Gikuyu to defend you."

"I have Ngai to defend me," Ma'muriuki said. "I will run to Ngai." She now felt certain that running away was exactly what Gichina wanted her to do. He would get that one wish, she decided.

"Our world has changed because of the Butterfly People," Ngeri said. "We have not yet seen these strangers among our clan, but we are not the same because of them. Because of them, too many ahoi from other clans live among us. They have no respect for Ngai and our traditions. When I was younger, I had never seen an ahoi, but now there are more of them than there are of us."

"This is true," Ma'muriuki said. "My shushu helped some ahoi in her home when I was a child, but they worked hard and purchased land and became true Gikuyu again. Today, there is no land to purchase."

"I see your son coming to talk to you," Ngeri said, looking out the door. She gestured to Muriuki, and then turned once more and put her hand on Ma'muriuki's arm. "You must do what is right for you. There are no true Gikuyu who would not understand." She stepped out of the hut and beckoned for Muriuki to go in and see his mother.

"Mama, we will be ready when it is time," Muriuki said as he knelt down next to his mother. "I talked to Wangari while we were working in the shamba. She will be ready."

"Good," Ma'muriuki said. "Makena is still too young to understand. Tonight or tomorrow night Gichina will come home drunk. We will leave early in the morning after he comes home so we can get away before he awakens."

"Mama, what will happen to the land we inherited from our father Waitimu?"

"My son, I do not know. A woman has no say in the matters of land. But Ngai will provide a way for you and your brother to get back what is rightfully yours. Those who took it did so at the risk of the curse of our ancestors and the anger of Ngai. The day will come, my son, but you must be patient, because you are not yet a man who can go to the elders for counsel."

Muriuki nodded. He had only three holes in his ears. It was not yet his time.

***

"Children, come quickly," Ma'muriuki whispered. "Our time has come."

They slipped quietly out of the enclosure. It had rained hard the night before, and she knew they must hurry to get across the river before the waters became too high to cross.

"Wait," whispered Ngeri, who had been following them. She embraced the children and then Ma'muriuki. "You have been good to me. I will pray often to Ngai for you."

"I hope when I am gone that there will be peace between you and Gichina," Ma'muriuki said.

"If not, I have a family to run to," Ngeri reminded her. "Now go. When he wakes up, I will delay him as long as I can so that he does not catch up with you."

"Thank you," Ma'muriuki said. "But I do not think he will follow us."

Ma'muriuki and the children slipped away in the early morning light. She had to get them across the river as soon as possible. She prayed to Ngai to keep the waters low until they had crossed.

She led the way, carrying Maathai. Her girls followed close behind her with Muriuki bringing up the rear. Ma'muriuki kept glancing back at him. He looked so big, strong, and protective. If their trip was successful, he would become a brave Maasai moran. She was so proud of him.

Just before they reached the river, she heard a scuffling sound behind her. She whirled around to see Gichina grab Muriuki and throw the struggling boy over his shoulder.

"Go, run," he said, "but this one stays with me. He will tend my livestock."

"Give my son back to me!" Ma'muriuki screamed. "He does not belong to you!"

She lunged at Gichina, but he was too strong for her. He gave her one last blow to her face and knocked her to the ground. By the time she got back on her feet, he was gone. Muriuki was gone. She looked in the direction of their disappearing forms, and then back at her two daughters and baby son. She sat on the ground and wept until there were no more tears.

"Come, children, we must hurry. The river is rising and we must cross it soon."

***

Ma'muriuki shuddered as she dipped her toe into the muddy water at the river's edge. It seemed like the best place to cross, but with the rains the night before, she did not know how deep it would be toward the middle, where the water was moving its fastest. She glanced back the way they had come. She did not see anyone, but she would not feel safe until the river was between her and the village. Her focus moved to her oldest daughter, Wangari, a few steps back. The young girl looked behind her and then into her mother's eyes. A flicker of fear showed in her face.

"Wait here, child. I will be back for you," she called to Wangari. She tightened the *ngoi* binding that wrapped her youngest child, Maathai, on her back. He whimpered, sensing his mother's concern. "Wangari, child, answer me when I call to you. Do you understand?"

"Yes, Mama," Wangari said. "I will wait for you." Wangari's eyes darted between her mother and the trail behind her. "Hurry, Mama."

"Good, child," Ma'muriuki said. She picked up her second daughter, Makena, and placed the wiggling little girl on her hip. "Still, child," she said, slapping the little girl's thigh sharply. Makena settled down immediately, and the young mother stepped into the river that had swollen overnight in the downpour. She could not go back now. She hoped to find shelter before nightfall in the home of a clan that lived across the river. After that, there would be no one left to guide her. She had only her understanding of the Gikuyu, distant memories of the Maasai, and Ngai to help her. Ma'muriuki remembered that her world had changed before, and change was not without hope.

She stepped into the cold water to cross the river and her world, once again, changed forever.

ABOUT THE AUTHOR

Skeeter Wilson was born in British Colonial East Africa, along the edge of the Gikuyu lands at the end of the Mau Mau War. The son of American missionaries, he witnessed Kenya's birth pangs as it became an independent nation. Wilson spent his early years divided between his Gikuyu friends and the children of expatriates at an American curriculum school.

Wilson lives in Auburn, Washington, and holds graduate degrees in creative fiction and African history.

Look for "Sons," Book Two in **The Agikuyu Series.**

Wilson's debut novel, **Worthless People**, is the story of Dave, a young man who grows up in Africa, knowing that one day he will have to leave the only home he knows and go to the America that his birth parents call home. His physical limitations prove an inconvenience to his out-of-touch parents, who work in Africa for foreign aid societies. But while they labor to rescue Africa from itself, Africa rescues Dave from his parents.

www.skeeterwilsonnovels.com

NOTES FROM THE AUTHOR

In modern Kenya, "Kikuyu" is the more common usage than "Gikuyu." I am not a linguist and have no stake in the proper spelling; however, the elders I spoke with preferred "Gikuyu," because they felt "Kikuyu" developed more from colonial and Swahili influences. Out of deference to these elders, I have adopted this spelling.

Pre-colonial Gikuyu people had a number of names for their concept of deity. The term "Ngai" used in this book is in more common use among modern Gikuyu than it was historically. For the sake of simplifying an already complex story, I chose to stay with this single term.

The description of the Gikuyu people in this novel and the following field notes may seem a little idealistic. In fact, it is. All cultures look at themselves and their history with a certain idealistic bias. Perhaps, in the future, I will complete and publish a manuscript in which I will examine the interviews more critically. However, it is their right to tell their story as they see it. And this is my attempt to tell their story the way I think they would want it told.

The following outline comes from field notes I took while doing interviews in Kenya in 2010. The details of *Crossing Rivers* come primarily from these interviews. Where historical works differed from my notes, I generally deferred to the perspective of those I interviewed.

FIELD NOTES

An Overview of the Gikuyu People

Anyone familiar with the migration patterns of the Bantu people will appreciate the difficulty of tracing the origins of the Gikuyu. However, it seems certain that, at least by the 1500s, the Gikuyu people were settled in a small area of what is now considered their land in the Kenyan highlands.

At that time, the Gikuyu were a minority culture, with the highlands occupied by three primary peoples: the Gumba (a pigmy people), the Athi, and the N'dorobo (also called Dorobo). The Gumba no longer exist. The Athi and N'dorobo have very complicated histories beyond the scope of this summary, but it may be helpful to understand that most modern N'dorobo are outcasts from neighboring cultures, and their connection to the original N'dorobo is difficult to determine.

Through a complex process of land purchase and assimilation, the Gikuyu expanded throughout the region and eventually became the majority culture of the area.

Gikuyu Names for Deity

Mugai: Literally means "server." The idea is that the source of everything is God.

Ngai: This is by far the most popular word for God in the current vernacular, but it seems this is more a matter of the adoption of this word for the Christian concept of God. The original source of "Ngai" is likely that it was borrowed from the Maasai deity word "Enkai."

This is the generic term for God and is sometimes used in conjunction with other deity words. For instance, there is a saying, *Ngai niwe Mugai*, which means "God is the only server," or "the source of all things is God." Here we see also the use of these two terms for the same deity. Historically, this confused early missionaries and anthropologists, who assumed that there were different gods rather than a variety of names for the same God.

Mwene Nyaga: Literally means "the owner of the spotted mountain," or "the owner of the ostrich," or "the owner of whiteness." The male ostrich is mostly black with large white areas toward its back; similarly, Kirinyaga (Mount Kenya), when seen from Gikuyu lands, is a mostly dark-to-black mountain with a white patch on its "backside." This has led many to conclude that the Gikuyu worshipped the mountain itself, which is not the case.

Murungu: Literally means "underworld dweller." Unlike Western beliefs, the underworld for the Gikuyu is not necessarily evil. The belief is that departed ancestors dwell beneath the roots of the sacred fig tree called the mugumo. Murungu visits the ancestors under the roots of this tree. It was an absolute taboo, in pre-colonial Gikuyu culture, to deface or cut down a mugumo tree.

The Two-Plus-One World View

The Gikuyu believed that there were three parts to existence, but in keeping with Gikuyu custom, they did not say "three" but rather they said "two plus" or "big two." (See the section "The nine-plus daughters" for an explanation of this custom.)

The first existence was the beforelife with Ngai. Ngai created all his children to live with him, and before humans were born to this earth, they enjoyed their existence with Ngai. The second existence was the afterlife, when all humans who had lived on the earth were called at their appointed time to return to Ngai and to once again enjoy their existence with their creator. The third existence was the very brief life on this earth between the first and the second. Ngai created the world for his pleasure and sends people to the earth to enjoy and take care of his world. The Gikuyu (and humans in general) were not from the earth. They were visitors who come from and belong with Ngai.

Origin Traditions

In the beginning. Mugai, the Creator of the Universe, was given special charge over a beautiful country surrounded by *Kirinyaga* (Mount Kenya), *Kia-Nyandarua* (the Aberdare Mountains), *Kia-Ng'ombe* (a hill now called Kiangombe), and *Kia-Mbiuiru* (the Ngong Hills).

Mugai put a rare white blanket of dust (snow) on Kirinyaga so that he could have a resting place when he came to visit the beautiful country. Mugai filled the land between these mountains with abundant trees and rivers and blessed it with good soil and rains. Mugai then made a man to look after the beautiful country, and he named the man Gikuyu (which means "large fig tree"). Mugai took Gikuyu to his resting place on top of Kirinyaga and showed him the land. Gikuyu was given authority over all the country and was told that it was his responsibility to take care of the beautiful land.

Before sending Gikuyu down the mountain, Mugai pointed in a direction to the south and told him there was a place on a ridge filled with fig trees (mukuyu) and a giant mukurwe tree. Mugai told Gikuyu that when he got to the place, he would recognize it, because on top of the giant tree there would be a bird called Nyagathanga. (The exact species of bird was not identifiable from this name, but Nyaga was a derivative of a deity word in Gikuyu culture. The bird was the symbol of the "spirit" or "messenger" of the deity, so a literal bird may not have been referenced.)

Mugai called the place *Mukurwe Wa Nyagathanga*. Gikuyu was instructed to build his homestead near the giant tree, and that when he was in need, he should make a sacrifice under a fig tree and lift his hands facing Kirinyaga, and Mugai would come to his assistance.

It took Gikuyu many difficult days of crossing rivers and climbing ridges as Mugai led him to the place of the fig trees. When he finally found the giant mukurwe, he was tired. He lay down under the tree and entered a deep sleep. When he awoke, he saw that Mugai had created a woman for him. Mugai told him the woman's name was Mumbi (which means "creator/provider").

The nine-plus daughters. Ngai gave Gikuyu and Mumbi nine daughters, plus one. In Agikuyu culture, it was considered prideful and arrogant to give an accurate accounting of one's blessings. For instance, a man with four goats would never say that he had four goats, for such arrogance might invite a bad ancestor to bring misfortune upon him. Instead, he would say that he had three-plus goats. And so it was with the daughters of Gikuyu. The Agikuyu do not say there were ten daughters of Gikuyu and Mumbi, but rather that they had "nine plus" or a "big nine." It was from these nine-plus daughters that the Gikuyu clans were divided. Each Agikuyu clan was named after one of the daughters. Even when others such as the Maasai or Akamba became part of the Agikuyu community, they could only do so by being adopted into one of the nine-plus clans.

The nine sons. Eventually the nine (or nine-plus, depending on the version) daughters grew older and told their mother they too deserved to make their own homes, but there were no men in the land to become their husbands. Mumbi reported the daughters' complaint to Gikuyu. He sent each girl into the forest to find a good stick that was her own height. When the daughters brought their sticks to Gikuyu, he took a ram and offered a sacrifice of petition to Mugai. He prayed for an answer as to how he was going to find nine-plus men to marry his daughters. As Gikuyu was praying, the voice of Mugai answered him in the sound of a thunderclap that was so loud Gikuyu fainted in fear. When he awoke, he saw nine (or nine-plus, depending on the version) men standing and waiting next to him. Gikuyu was amazed that his prayer was answered. He led the men to his daughters, who were very happy when they met the man that Mugai had given each of them. Some traditions state that, in the thunder, Mugai divided a part of himself to make the husbands for the daughters.

In some versions of the story, the last daughter was too young to marry. In other versions, she was stated to be an illegitimate daughter.

When women ruled. Initially, women ruled men, because they were the daughters of the first nine-plus daughters, and because they were the givers of life. However, the women ruled the men harshly, and their demands were cruel. The men gathered to discuss the matter. They decided that each of them would go to their wife's hut on the same night, and all would get their wives pregnant on the same day. When the wives were heavy with child, the men rebelled and have ruled ever since.

Wild animals and iron. Mugai divided his animals, giving some to men and some to women. The women had only sharp sticks and wooden knives for slaughtering their animals for food. The animals suffered greatly, displeasing Ngai, so he made the women's animals wild and untamable. When the men saw what Ngai had done to the women's animals, they feared that he would do the same to theirs. They went to the mountain of Ngai and offered a sacrifice and prayers asking for guidance so that they did not lose the animals that Ngai had given them. Ngai was very pleased that the men had sought his advice. He told them to follow the river until they reached the place of black sand. He instructed them to take the sand, heat it, pour the metal that comes out of the sand into molds, and make knives so they could slaughter their animals without cruelty. The men rejoiced and thanked Ngai, who told them they must be kind to the women and share the meat from their animals with them.

As a sign of this promise, women shared a portion of the men's meat, and a man was not allowed to eat the kidneys and liver, as these were reserved for women. Since this time it has been considered irresponsible and lazy to kill a wild animal, because they were women's food that were set free by Ngai.

No one could remain a Gikuyu for long if it was found that they killed wild animals for food. Such a person would be banished from the people and would join the N'dorobo.

Land

The significance of land. One can only understand the traditional Gikuyu concept of land if they understand the Gikuyu concept of Ngai. It was Ngai who showed them the land between the great mountains and sent them to take care of it and make it productive. These tasks were essential to their identification as a people. The more land a man owned and managed responsibly, the more evidence of his blessing from Ngai.

Perhaps a comparison could be made with the neighboring Maasai. A traditional Maasai was defined by ownership of healthy cattle; indeed, their belief that Enkai gave all cattle to them was so strong, they considered their raids on their neighbors (such as the Gikuyu) in which they "stole" cattle not a matter of theft but rather a return of what was properly theirs. One could not remain a Maasai for long if they had lost their cattle; instead, they became part of the N'dorobo. In a similar way, a true Gikuyu was a landowner, and prior to colonialism, there were few exceptions to this.

The Gikuyu concept of land ownership. The Gikuyu's rights and responsibilities to work the land were based on the blessings of Ngai for their hard labor. It was unheard of to give up land or sell it to another Gikuyu, and in the absence of deceit, it was unlikely that a Gikuyu would lose the land he had acquired. This did not preclude the possibility of land exchanges, only that a Gikuyu did not give up what Ngai has given him responsibility over. For much of the Gikuyu's existence, they were not the only occupants of the land between the mountains. The primary occupants were the N'dorobo, the Athi, and a small forest people called the Gumba. Even the Maasai occupied some of the lands. Fortunately, none of their neighbors had the same strong territorial inclinations as the Gikuyu. As they grew in numbers, they were able to purchase new land for farming from their co-occupants. It was the manifest destiny of the Gikuyu to eventually inhabit the entire area that Ngai had given them.

The landless. A landless Gikuyu, called an *ahoi*, became a tenant farmer on the property of a Gikuyu landowner. As long as an ahoi was a responsible and productive farmer, there was no explicit shame in their position; however, it was the goal of every ahoi to accumulate sufficient goats and sheep to purchase land for themselves in order to give their offspring a legacy. It was a burden and a humiliation for a father to not have the means to pass on property to his sons. If an ahoi did not demonstrate an effort to gain land by becoming a tenant farmer, or if the ahoi chose instead to hunt wild animals, he was no longer considered Gikuyu but N'dorobo.

Land purchasing. A Gikuyu did not believe that land taken by force was, in fact, their land. To be legitimate owners, they had to purchase the land from a Maasai, an ahoi, or others by a very carefully orchestrated ceremony. If, for instance, they purchased land from the Maasai, a ceremony was necessary to make the Maasai a Gikuyu and the Gikuyu a Maasai. This way the rules of both cultures would recognize the permanent nature of the sale. The sale would always involve an exchange of cattle and sheep or goats, which was the currency among them. It would be done in the presence of a council of Gikuyu elders, who would formally affirm the legitimacy and permanence of the boundaries of the exchange. Boundaries would be made up of natural land features such as streams, ridges, and cliffs, and on occasion, certain types of ceremonial trees that could never be cut down. Often the purchase would include the seller marrying one of the purchaser's daughters, but all children of the marriage would be considered Gikuyu. The Gikuyu assimilated many other cultures into their numbers, and land purchasing was one of the primary ways this happened. The Gumba seem to have simply disappeared just before the colonial era. One theory holds that they were completely assimilated into the Gikuyu culture by marriage and land purchase agreements.

Land and wealth. A wealthy person would usually have extensive land holdings and often would have extended family and ahoi living and working on their land. Such a person had absolute rights over his land and, as such, were the closest the Gikuyu had to the concept of a "chief" or "big man." However, the power of a wealthy person was limited to the borders of their own land and whatever position they may have held on the local council of elders.

Because land was purchased but not sold to other Gikuyu, the ownership of cattle, sheep, and goats was the true indication of wealth. Without these, there was no possibility of marriage, payment to elders for legal proceedings, purchase of land, or status among the other clans.

Livestock as the cause of conflict. Gikuyu were farmers, not herders, and as long as relations were peaceful with their neighbors, their uncircumcised boys were the primary caretakers of the livestock.

The Maasai, on the other hand, considered the Gikuyu livestock to belong to them. As a necessary part of recognition, Maasai warriors conducted raids into the Gikuyu lands to steal livestock (or, in their view, return what was rightfully theirs). Unlike the Maasai, the Gikuyu were not a warrior-centric people. However, a newly circumcised man became a warrior assigned to protect the tribe against such invasions as those by the Maasai.

The reality was that these were not really wars between the Gikuyu and the Maasai. They were, instead, local conflicts that were settled locally. Such a conflict could easily be occurring in one place while peaceful trading took place on the next ridge. The Gikuyu women had a saying: "While our men fight the Maasai, the women trade with them." Ultimately, the mutual benefit of trade far outweighed allowing the local conflicts to become larger.

Inheritance. Land and livestock were passed on equally to sons (including adopted sons). Women had no land ownership rights; however, a widow always had the right to live on a small plot of land with her own farm and livestock, supported by her children, for as long as she lived. Mothers were much more highly revered than fathers in Gikuyu culture, and the mistreatment of a mother was among the most grievous of wrongdoings in the culture.

Judicial System

According to Gikuyu legend, when men took over rule of the people from women, they established a system of chiefs similar to what they observed in the neighboring peoples. A few generations after the first man named Gikuyu, a second man with the same name (sometimes referred to as King Gikuyu) became the ruling chief. However, he ruled with such cruel tyranny that a *rika* of men called the "revolters" overthrew him. (The word "rika" is explained under "Stages of Life.")

The people decided they no longer wanted a "chieftain" system. Instead, each man among the Gikuyu would go through a series of maturation steps, and with each step, he would participate more in the responsibility of government. This new system resulted in a balance between the self-reliance of each household (or subclan) and the judicial system of an ever-maturing eldership of men from across all clans. What resulted was a system of limited self-rule within the bounds of the culture and the judicial constraints of the elders.

The elders did not have a police or military for enforcement; this idea was foreign. Instead, the people went to the elders for rulings and arbitrations in the event of a dispute or unjust action. There were four levels of elders (explained later) that could act as a court of appeals for more serious disputes or issues that affected the people at large.

Cases of murder. There was no differentiation in Gikuyu culture between murder and accidental death. A death was a death, and the clan or family members of the deceased would go to the clan of the person responsible and demand compensation. This would be done in the presence of the elders, who would hear the facts and oversee the compensation. The death of a male was always one hundred sheep in payment to the bereaved family, and the death of a female was always sixty goats. There was never a question as to why the death occurred except for establishing the responsible party. These payments were very taxing on the wealth of the clan required to make the payment. But pay they did, and if they were a poor clan and could not afford the payment, they would become indebted to stronger clans for the balance of what they could not pay.

Because everyone paid so dearly for a death, there was extreme social caution about any potential situation that might cause injury to another. If, in a rare case, the same person caused the death of a second person, the clan may choose to make the payment, but if the clan decided that the person in question was of bad character, they had the option after the second or third death to turn the offending party over to the other clan. In most cases, such a person would be killed by the bereaved clan members.

While the concession was made that it was theoretically possible the same person could be involved in the death of two people, it was also asserted that such a thing was so rare as to be almost unheard of.

This then, is how the judicial system worked. Every action that caused harm had a required compensation that was overseen by the elders and for which the clan, rather than the individual, paid the consequence. Once the payment was made, no matter how large or small, the clan member was returned to his or her normal position within the clan with no additional consequences. The matter was settled and forgotten.

Governing by taboo. There were many taboos in Gikuyu culture, each of which had predetermined consequences. Many taboos were related to farming. For instance, it was taboo to step under a banana tree. The fine was the payment of a goat or a ram. Most of such taboos had practical reasons. As bananas ripened, the green cluster was supported by wooden stakes. A person walking under a banana tree could disturb the stakes and ruin the harvest. The taboo was designed to protect farmers from the carelessness of others.

Another example was harvesting food from another person's farm. If a traveler was hungry and passing a farm, they could freely enter and pick food to eat. As long as they were within the confines of the farm, they could eat what they wanted and then continue on their journey without consequence. However, if they took any food with them outside the farm, they were considered thieves and were fined heavily.

Most taboos were designed to regulate and modify behavior for what was perceived the common good. Others dealt more directly with the Gikuyu belief system and fear of angering the ancestors.

Stages of Life

Rika. The age set or *rika*, as it was called among the Gikuyu, is fundamental to understanding Gikuyu society and structure. Every person, especially from circumcision onward, became part of an age group with whom they associated and worked together for the rest of their lives. Together they became warriors, went to courting dances, got married, had children, became elders, took over the judicial duties, and even expected to die and join the ancestors in proximity to each other. This age set was the glue that held the Gikuyu people together; it crossed all clans and was an unshakable fraternity.

A society of secrets. This is a very complex subject that could become an entire study in itself. Simplistically, as a person enters a new stage of life, they were given a new level of cultural secrets in an oathing ceremony. If they revealed any secret to one who was not in the same stage as them, they did so at the risk of their life. As one can well imagine, there was a myriad of myths and half-truths both within and outside the Gikuyu world about the nature of these secrets.

Children as a blessing from Ngai. Children belonged to Ngai before they were sent to this earth as a blessing to their parents. A mother and father had no ownership of their children, only the responsibility as caretakers of Ngai's children, just as they were caretakers of Ngai's earth.

It was very important to a Gikuyu to have at least one son, so that there was someone to inherit the land. Beyond this, there was little preference for having male or female children, as there were considerable benefits to both. The ideal Gikuyu family had two boys and two girls, as it was believed that the children carried with them the spirits of their grandparents. The firstborn boy was named after the paternal grandfather, the firstborn girl, the paternal grandmother. The second boy was named after the maternal grandfather and the second girl after the maternal grandmother. Because there was some fear of offending the ancestors, every parent desired a child to carry on the spirit of their parents after they had gone to the next life. So four children was a complete family, but more was better, and each boy or girl born was alternatively named after the next nearest relative to their maternal or paternal grandparents.

Childbirth. When a mother was in labor, she was attended by her mother, if possible, along with female relatives and a midwife. The husband and other related males sat in silence outside the woman's hut waiting for news.

After a child was born, the midwife checked to be certain he or she was alive. If it was a boy, they gave five loud ululations (in this case, celebratory screams) as an announcement that a boy had been born, and the father received congratulations that the "owner of the house has come home." If the child was a girl, four ululations were given, and the father received congratulations that the "giver and supporter of life has come home."

The infant stayed in the exclusive care of the mother for

eight days. If the child died during that period, he or she was buried quietly and in hiding by the mother. The child was considered an integral extension of the mother for those eight days. On the ninth day, the baby was presented to the father, and a goat was taken to the elders for a sacrifice of thanksgiving to Ngai. After the eighth day, it was the father who buried a child who died.

A child nursed, from its mother's breast as long as he or she was willing to suckle. It was considered a curse on the child to drink milk from another mother, or to drink the milk of a cow or goat, while still nursing. The mother would begin to introduce food by chewing fruit and vegetables and placing the chewed food in the baby's mouth.

Education. It was the responsibility of the mother and the grandparents to give the children their basic education, which centered primarily on stories designed to teach the values and traditions of the Gikuyu.

Uncircumcised boys. By the age of five or six, a young boy would begin to take care of livestock along with the older boys. He would spend most of his pre-circumcision life raising livestock and occasionally following his father in other duties.

Play time involved practicing two important skill sets: leadership skills and fighting skills. Each boy who was so inclined claimed a leadership role in the responsibilities of caring for the livestock and developing warrior-type fighting skills.

There were two very important elements of leadership. First, the boy had to demonstrate the ability to lead and motivate the group in a way that was to the benefit of all. There could be no evidence of favoritism or self-benefit from the leader. Second, the followers had to demonstrate fidelity to the leader and absolute comradeship with the entire group. One who did not lead well was replaced, and one who did not follow well was not allowed to lead. After circumcision, when the boys became warriors and eventually elders, the leaders were often chosen from these childhood games, so this play time was taken very seriously.

Unlike the Maasai, the Gikuyu did not see themselves as a warrior culture. They were farmers, and their warriors existed primarily as a defensive necessity against outside invaders. On the other hand, the Gikuyu were very fierce defensive fighters, and warriors were expected to have the basic skill sets to perform well in the event of an invasion. It was the responsibility of boys to develop the basic skills to be ready to become warriors.

One game used to develop these skills involved making bows and arrows and wooden spears. The boys would practice building these weapons until each boy had a useful set. One boy would bend a long, green stick into a circle so that it would roll along the ground. He would then roll the loop in front of the other boys while they took turns trying to shoot an arrow or throw a spear through it. The boy with the most successful attempts would replace the one rolling the loop until another boy's skills exceeded his, and then he would be replaced as well.

Young boys spent their first few years sleeping in their mother's house in an area also designated for the goats. It was well known when they were at this stage of development, because they smelled of goat urine. After they become a little older, they might move temporarily into their father's hut but soon they were expected to fend for themselves, often building temporary huts for each other.

Uncircumcised girls. Uncircumcised girls stayed in their mother's house until circumcision and, in some cases, until marriage. Their duties were to work with their mother, learning her skill sets. On rare occasions a girl may also help out with the care of livestock, but her primary duties were working in the garden and learning how to prepare food and drink. Because of the extensive interaction between mothers, grandmothers, and daughters, young girls were the best equipped to understand Gikuyu traditions and to pass them on to their own children.

Sex play. It was accepted for there to be some sex play between uncircumcised girls and boys. The extent or acceptability of this play is a matter of debate among modern Gikuyu. As the girls approached menstruation, however, this sex play became increasingly taboo.

Approaching reason. A mother looked for certain signs of maturity among her children. Generally, this meant the ability to reason rather than physical maturity. What these signs were are unclear, but they typically developed between seven and ten years of age (seven for girls and ten for boys). When a mother determined that the age of maturity had been reached, she grabbed her child firmly by the ear and pierced a hole in the upper lobe with a large thorn. The first time this happened, the child often screamed in pain and surprise, but the mother prevented any removal of the thorn. After a week or two the hole stopped festering and the mother removed the thorn and replaced it with a small stick to keep it open.

Each year at about the same time, the mother repeated this process, until there were six holes (three in each ear). The year after the sixth hole was placed in the ear, the child was deemed ready for circumcision.

The necessity of circumcision. As with many African cultures, circumcision was the most crucial rite of passage in the life of a Gikuyu. Without circumcision a person never achieved adulthood, could never marry, and would earn no protection or community status. A person who refused circumcision (an almost unheard-of event) would be banished from the community and probably would not be able to gain entrance to other communities, including the N'dorobo.

The act of circumcision. The time and year of circumcisions was determined by a council of elders who had gathered from the various clans. Issues such as famine, war, or other disasters may put off the circumcision rite for a year or, under extreme circumstances, several years. Ideally, a girl was circumcised just before menstruation began and a boy at about age fifteen. If a girl had her menstruation before her circumcision, she was considered to be ceremonially unclean, and a goat must be sacrificed on her behalf before she could undergo the ritual.

Sponsors. Each candidate for circumcision was assigned sponsors. The sponsors were an older couple who would see the candidate through the process. They became lifelong mentors after the circumcision, so they were chosen carefully. The parents chose the sponsors, but the child could overrule their choice and even choose their own couple.

Eight days. In most cases, the boys in a given area stayed together in one or two huts during an eight-day period of exclusion from the community. Eight days was often understood to be a time of rebirth. During the exclusion, the boys' food was delivered by their sponsors. The boys were not allowed to talk to or look at their mothers during this time, even if they went outside to relieve themselves. Girls, on the other hand, remained in exclusion in their mother's home, but they too were fed and cared for by their sponsors.

The location. Circumcisions always occurred early in the morning under the shade of the sacred mugumo tree, which was always located near a large stream or river. The boys and girls were covered with ceremonial sheep grease and walked naked to the river with a white cloth on their arms and a green branch broken from a tree. As they approached the river, younger children would line along the way, mocking them and their appearance. Once they came out of the river, no child could ever mock them again.

The boys and girls walked into the river as deep as possible, or at least deep enough to cover their genitalia. At this point they would throw their branches and watch them float down the river. This symbolized that a once-living child was dead. The early morning river was very cold, and this had the effect of anesthetizing their genitalia to a limited degree before circumcision.

The circumcision of boys. Boys would sit in a row under the mugumo tree, completely naked. They sat with their feet wide apart and their arms supporting them on the ground behind them. Their family and neighbors would crowd close and watch the boys faces for any sign of fear or show of pain during the surgery.

The surgeon, standing among the crowd, would begin to chant. He would be dressed in a brilliant display of feathers and a variety of pigments were painted on his skin. The crowd would part for his approach. The surgeon would first count the boys to be certain that there was an even number, as an odd number of candidates would spell a certain bad omen on the proceedings. If necessary, one of the boys would be removed and required to wait until the next circumcision date.

The surgeon would start at one end and work quickly down the line of boys. He would grab the foreskin and pull it over the penis head, make the cut, and move to the next boy. The boy was expected to sit in unflinching silence through his own procedure and as the other boys were cut. The surgeon then would return to the first boy and shave off any jagged edges of the foreskin. If the crowd approved of the boy's behavior, they would cheer and begin songs of bravery; if he failed by flinching or crying, they sang songs of mockery. A boy's status as a warrior and his likelihood of finding a wife during his warrior years largely hinged on this single event.

As soon as the surgeon was finished, the male sponsor would carefully wrap the wound with a white cloth and lead the boy back to the hut where he would stay in seclusion until the wound healed. Healing may have taken from one to six months. There was no attempt to stop the bleeding, nor was antiseptic applied, so infections were common. The male sponsor would bring food and gifts from the family and was the only one allowed to look at the wound, which he did regularly. If the healing was slow, he gave advice on how to speed up healing, though he made no attempt to directly interfere with the healing process.

The circumcision of girls. The process for the girls was similar to the boys in that an even number lined up with their legs wide apart on the grass under the mugumo tree. The girl's woman sponsor would sit behind and hold the girl in position for the surgery. The surgeon for the girls was always a woman. She pressed on either side of the clitoris and cut off the exposed portion of the clitoris and tips of the labia. She then went down the line but did not return after the initial cut. The girls were expected to remain as stoic and brave as possible during the procedure, but there was no shame or mockery if they did cry out or show pain. The girls returned to their mother's hut and remained in seclusion until they heal, but they were still attended by their female sponsor for the duration of the recovery.

The sponsors as mentors. As mentioned above, the sponsors remain the lifelong mentors of the now-circumcised adults. They were allowed to be the sponsors of more than one candidate at the same time. The man looked after the boys under their care and the woman, the girls. During the entire recovery process, the sponsors were not permitted to engage in any sexual acts, or there would be a bad omen placed on those under their care.

Courtship and dances. Every new initiate across all the Gikuyu clans was in the same rika as the other adults circumcised on that same day. It was a strict taboo for persons to marry within the same clan, no matter how distant the blood line may actually be. Therefore, it was necessary for them to meet members of the opposite sex from other clans.

Across the Gikuyu lands, wealthy landowners set aside areas on their land for dances. During times of relative peace, groups of age mates gathered regularly at various dances, giving them the opportunity to meet up with others their same age. Generally, marriage did not occur for several years after circumcision, so there was a significant amount of time available for them to become acquainted and form bonds.

Despite the mockery of a boy who shows pain at circumcision, the Gikuyu were very careful not to bring shame on each other. The same was true of couples at the courtship dances. If a man was interested in a woman during a dance, he would casually put his hand on her shoulder. If she felt the same, she put her hand on his shoulder and stepped on his feet to let him know the interest was mutual. If she did not do this, there was no spectacle; he was expected not to attempt further connection with her and to seek another woman. While the two were getting to know each other, either may end the relationship by not putting their arm on the shoulder of the other person during the next dance. No words were exchanged, and the relationship was over.

During the dancing festivals, a group of young men and women would sometimes agree to sleep in the same hut. Couples who had paired off may also choose to sleep in a hut by themselves. The females were carefully bound around their genital area to prevent access by the males.

The cultural taboo against unmarried pregnancy was so strong and the consequences to the family and clan so great (a fine by the elders of sheep and goats for the loss of virginity), such pregnancies were almost unheard of.

Young warrior/older warrior. Between circumcision and early marriage was the period when all men were warriors. As the older warriors married and moved into early eldership, the next rika moved up in status and the rika groups behind them became increasingly under their control. Infrequently, when a young warrior showed exceptional skill or bravery in a fight, he could be included in some of the activities above him. However, this did not mean that he moved up from his own rika, only that his status in his rika was enhanced.

The Gikuyu devised a series of defensive measures such as war pits—a hole built on a path with a series of stakes

CROSSING RIVERS

designed to impale an advancing enemy. They built bridge systems across their rivers that made use of the natural foliage and were designed to be undetected by their enemies. Maasai in particular had an aversion to water. They did not swim nor willingly crossed water any deeper than the waist. Communities near the Maasai lands were fortified and well hidden. Even on trading routes, it was said that a person could walk within feet of a Gikuyu compound and never know it.

The general defensive strategy for the Gikuyu was simple but effective. If a community was under attack by outsiders (usually Maasai), the warriors would make a defensive stand designed not to stop them from stealing their animals as much as to slow them down. At the same time, the women, children, and older men would scatter into the woods and sound a distress cry to the surrounding compounds. Warriors from the other compounds would not come to the aid of the attacked compound; rather, they would go behind the attackers and set traps along the return paths and then lie in wait for the retreating Maasai with the livestock. The goal of the warriors under attack was only to hold off the Maasai until the traps were set and then disappear into the woods.

The retrieval of stolen livestock very likely followed this same method, so the Gikuyu tried to avoid any direct engagement with the more sophisticated Maasai warriors. Usually, the Gikuyu warriors would plan an attack on a Maasai herd in retaliation, regardless of the success of the Maasai raid. The young warriors relished these raids, as they gave them the opportunity to demonstrate bravery and improve their status in the community. A successful retaliation resulted in the return of any stolen livestock and the taking of additional livestock as compensation for their trouble. Based on individual bravery, the warriors took the best of the livestock to build their own herds and shared the rest with their communities.

Marriage. For the Gikuyu, marriage, like the rika (age set)

181

system, was one of the primary ways that the people were bound together. Marriage was a way of creating alliances with families in other clans and making the household a stronger and more influential part of the community. A successful marriage benefited the entire clan. The primary definition of an unsuccessful marriage was the absence of children. The wife was usually assumed to be at fault; however, the husband was free to take another wife (if he could afford to) and prove that the problem did not lie with him. If it was demonstrated that the wife was to blame, the husband could, if he chose, send her back to her family and demand the return of her dowry. In most cases, the husband would likely keep the wife, especially if she was the first wife, and perhaps demand some of the dowry back.

It was unusual for a wife to leave her husband, but if she did, she would be required to return to her family. The most likely reason would be physical abuse, but the husband could still demand the repayment of her dowry. But her family could also demand payment from him if abuse was evident. Once a separation occurred, the Gikuyu people recognized it as a divorce. There was no place for an unmarried woman in Gikuyu culture, and while the woman who left her husband would be free to remarry, she would have great difficulty finding another husband. Most likely she would become a third or fourth wife to a wealthier man who needed an extra worker in his fields.

Process of marriage proposal. By the time a warrior reached the age where his rika has begun to marry, he had likely come to know through the many cultural dancing opportunities the woman he wanted to wed. But in keeping with the Gikuyu determination of not shaming anyone, the process was such that it clarified with certainty that the woman was mutually interested in him.

While there were several variations, the most common method of proposal was a three-step system designed to avoid public shame.

The first step involved a visit to the hut of the mother by three or four men from the same rika and clan, including the one who wanted to marry the woman's daughter. The mother would invite them in, knowing that there was only one reason why several men from the same rika as her daughter would be visiting. One of the men would tell the daughter that they came to talk of marriage. If she was willing to discuss the matter, she would say that she was unable to marry so many men, or, if she was not interested in any of the visitors, she would say that it was not a matter for her to decide. The mother would immediately visit the father in his hut and tell him that some men from a certain clan were visiting his daughter.

It was the father's duty to know the various clans and whether there was any reason why his daughter should not or could not marry someone from the visiting clan. Unless there was a ban against marrying someone from the boy's clan, the father would give his approval to the mother. If he did not approve, the mother would then carry drinks back and give them to the men from the rejected clan. If the father approved, the mother would return empty-handed and the daughter would serve them drinks to indicate her acceptance.

The second step occurred after the son went back and informed his father that he had found someone he wished to marry. If the son's father approved of the potential marriage, he went with his son to the hut of the girl's father. The three men discussed many things and talked about their families and land holdings, since it was likely they had never met before. Finally, the son's father told the woman's father that his son would like to plant a farm in the other man's field. The man would reply that he had enough wives and daughters to work in his field and did not need help from the man's son. All parties knew, of course, exactly what was going on. The son's father would say that his son wanted to farm in a very important field that belonged to the other man. The daughter's father would then call out to her to bring the men drinks. The daughter would bring in gourds filled usually with a bitter gruel made from fermented grains. She would pass a drink to the two fathers and then one to the son. If she took a sip of the gruel before handing it to the son, it meant she was in agreement. If she handed the drink to him without taking a sip, it meant she was not in agreement. If she did not sip the gruel, the men continued to talk as if nothing had happened and the father and son left without any shame. On the other hand, if the daughter sipped the gruel, then the second step was complete, and all parties knew it was time to negotiate the dowry.

The third step was the negotiation ceremony between the fathers and the most important relatives from both families. A goat was always roasted and substantial amounts of honey beer made, all supplied by the son's family.

Negotiations could be tricky and were not always successful. But if both the son and daughter were determined, the fathers would usually find some way of working things out. In cases where the son's family was too poor to afford a dowry, the daughter's father could still accept the marriage. In such a case, the son moved onto the land of the daughter's father, and any children she bore for her husband belonged to her clan instead of him. However, if he gained enough personal wealth (cattle, sheep, and goats), he could begin to make payments and move back to his own land with his father, and the children then became part of his clan.

The steps of making dowry payments were many and began immediately. It was very common for a husband to continue to make dowry payments for many years. The payments always included the delivery of goats (usually four at a time). Initially, the payments were made with great ceremony and gatherings of clan members from both sides. The purpose was to get to know each other and to cement long-term relationships.

The wedding. The wedding date, set by the fathers, was kept hidden from the bride-to-be; though, she knows when it was near, because she was required go into a hut for eight days of seclusion before she could marry. Like the period prior to circumcision, the eight days signified the death of her old life in her clan; the marriage signified the birth of her life in the new clan. During the eight days, she was kept company by friends whom she might not see again, particularly in the case of a distant clan marriage.

While the bride-to-be was in seclusion, the families of the groom-to-be build the new couple's hut or huts. This was done in one day; an average hut would last about five years before rebuilding or repairs were necessary. The groom then waited for his bride in the new home. There were specific furnishings such as beds, fire stones, and starter livestock that were supplied by the fathers of both clans.

On the ninth day, or soon after, a group of men from the groom's clan come to the bride's hut and "kidnapped" her. She screamed, fought, and called out that she was being stolen from her father. She yelled for people to save her; it was an act that was rehearsed since childhood. It was a way of showing her sorrow for being torn apart from her family and the loss for both her and them.

When she arrived at her new home, she would be led to her hut to meet her new husband. The wedding was complete.

The marriage duties. There was clear division of labor and responsibilities between a husband and wife; however, both were expected to have at least a nominal understanding of each other's duties. The husband owned the land, and the woman owned the homestead. It was improper for either of them to interfere with the other's domain, though mutual support in times of need or sickness was expected of both. The children were raised by the mother, and she planted and tended the farm along with her young sons and daughters. Generally, the husband did not do any daily farming but was still in charge of certain perennial crops.

The husband's main responsibilities were the livestock and breaking new ground for farming. As the wealth of the family was dependent on the accumulation of crops and livestock, the need for breaking new ground or negotiating the purchase of additional lands for production never ended. Early in the marriage, the husband would still be called upon as a warrior if a conflict escalated, but this occurred less as his family grew. While the wife had no livestock duties, she did have control over a steady supply of goats, which were usually kept in her hut for fattening, as fattened goats were in constant demand with the many celebrations and sacrifices in Gikuyu life.

The home. The most basic Gikuyu compound had two huts—one for the woman, goats for fattening, daughters, and very young sons, and one for her husband. Older sons fended for themselves or built a temporary shelter behind the mother's hut. The woman's hut had the wedding bed, which was the only place that the Gikuyu people accepted sexual activity. This was true even when the hut was filled with children and goats. The man's hut had a small room or ledge for his bed, and the rest was an open area with benches and three legged stools. All the negotiations and meetings with visitors were carried out in the husband's hut while all family activities took place in the wife's hut.

A Gikuyu hut was roughly sixteen feet in diameter, but this could vary greatly depending on the size or number of occupants. In addition to the two occupied huts, there were one or two elevated grain huts, usually sitting next to the wife's hut for storing produce from the field.

Four stages of eldership. When the first child of a married couple was circumcised, the husband became eligible to be a first-level elder in his clan. In order to become an elder, two goats needed to be offered. The first goat was usually given to the elders by the man's father while the man was still a child or a warrior. This did not always happen, however, and the man may be required to supply the first goat himself. The second goat was given to the elders at an initiation ceremony.

Gikuyu culture was a culture of secrets—this becomes

most apparent as one enters the world of eldership. With each stage, the elder learned information about his people that was kept from all other Gikuyu.

The first level of eldership was a sort of elder-in-training stage. Second- and third-level elders used first-level elders as messengers between the different clans. Some of the messages were of vital importance to the clans; others were simply tests to see if the first-level elder could be trusted to accurately transmit information. Being an oral culture, trades and communications needed to be done by messenger, and it was critical that such messages be sent and received accurately. Every first-level elder was expected to graduate to the second level after a number of years, but the ones who had more difficulty transmitting information were in for more rigorous and sometimes miserable testing by their seniors.

The second-level elder was allowed to sit on the clan councils and participate in the local judicial decisions. He also had to present goats to the elders above him and wait for them to promote him to the second level. Usually an elder was not promoted until the majority of men in his rika were ready to be promoted as well.

The third-level elders sat on councils that negotiated or made decisions that affected relationships between each clan. They settle disputes within the clan, cases of homicide, and border disputes. During this period, these elders began to be divided into two groups. Those who demonstrated administrative skills were tutored by the fourth-level elders to be on the supreme council. Those who showed more spiritual inclinations were tutored by those fourth-level elders who made sacrifices to Ngai, prayed on behalf of the people, practiced deeper levels of medicine, and officiated at ceremonies.

Those in the fourth and final stage of eldership were the statesmen of the Gikuyu people. They were the spiritual and judicial heads. Few cases made it to the fourth level, but when a case did so, the fourth-level elders' decisions were final and indisputable. For the most part, these men were well advanced in years and acted as advisors and mentors for the other elders in the clans. They were highly respected by everyone.

Stages of motherhood. With rare exceptions, married women did not have judicial responsibilities and did not engage in any elder-type functions. They had three basic stages of life. In the first stage, as a new wife, they were addressed as "daughter of..." and the name of their mother was supplied. Their personal name was seldom or never used until they had children old enough to be married themselves. Once they bore their first child, their name became "mother of..." and the name of the firstborn child was inserted. When they had grandchildren, they were then called Shushu, or "grandmother." This was the highest honor. Everyone, especially sons, gave deference to their mothers. Next to the neglect of Ngai, the neglect or shaming of a mother was one of the most grievous wrongs a man could commit in Gikuyu culture. As a shushu became advanced in years, her advice was sought by younger men and women as often as that of the fourth-level elders. Some shushus eventually became very powerful influences in the community as a result, and their advice or demands were almost never denied.

Death. Death was the subject of widest variance in my interviews. The Gikuyu people looked forward to death with great optimism. They had a steadfast belief in the afterlife—they came from Ngai and they returned to Ngai. They also had an enduring belief that the spirits of the ancestors remained around them at all times. This awareness was so acute that it was not unusual for there to be dialogue (or at least a monologue) with the ancestors. They did not worship ancestors, because they believed in the worship of Ngai only; however, they did believe in the influence of the spirits of good and bad ancestors, including curses for certain kinds of misbehaviors.

It would be wrong to interpret this as some sort of death cult. There was no focus on death; in fact, it was quite the contrary. Death was just not considered to be a big deal. A very old person who lived beyond most or all of their known age mates would feel like they had been forgotten, and supplications might even be made to Ngai asking why they had not been taken along with their rika.

On the other hand, the touching of a dead body was considered a taboo, and a person who accidentally or by necessity touched a dead body was required to take goats to the elders for sacrifices to remove the uncleanness and any ancestral curses from themselves.

A landowner who knew he was dying would call his sons to him and give them his last instructions. His eldest son was usually the administrator of the estate, unless he had disqualified himself. However, the administrator was simply an administrator among equals, and his only right was to carry out the wishes of his father.

The dying father would be carried to a temporary hut near the place where he wished to be buried on his property. His sons would then establish a death watch, taking turns making him comfortable and watching to see if he would recover. If he did die, he would be carried to a predug hole, which would be filled with soil and piled over with rocks. The temporary hut would be burned to the ground. If the father (or any other family member) died unexpectedly in one of the other huts, that hut would be burned and a new one constructed on a different site. No one knowingly built any hut over the site of a person's death.

A mother or daughter would be allowed to die in their own hut. After all, the compound belonged to the women. They would be buried in the same manner as the father in a designated area. If the mother died and there were daughters in the hut, the daughters would be adopted by other wives or, in rare cases, relatives, and the hut would be burned.

If a man was still in the warrior stage and owned no land or was an ahoi (landless Gikuyu), they would not be buried but left for the hyenas to carry them off. If they died in an unsightly area, they would be thrown into bushes or somewhere away from public view. If a warrior died in a fight, his body was left and an artifact such as his spear or bow would be brought back to his relatives. His body would be left where he died for the hyenas.

The Gikuyu were a people of the land, and only those who owned land and cultivated it responsibly were buried in the earth that the Gikuyu were given by Ngai.

END NOTES

I am painfully aware of how much of what I learned from the elders remains unstated in this overview. It is an impossible task to describe, much less understand, a vanishing culture. Modern Gikuyu do not practice many of the traditions mentioned in the preceding section; in fact, it seems safe to say that many contemporary Gikuyu are not aware of most of these traditions mentioned. A century of misinformation by colonialism, missionaries, and post-independence notions of a tribal-free Kenya has made much of the Gikuyu past a distant memory. Modernity has a way of making people want to forget their past, something future generations may well regret. It seems to me that the Gikuyu people have an amazing and sophisticated history, and it is well worth preserving these memories and passing them on to their children.

Additional Reading

Cagnolo, C. *The Akikuyu: Their Customs, Traditions and Folklore*. Nyrie: Mission Printing School, 1933.

Lambert, H.E. *Kikuyu Social and Political Institutions*. London: Oxford University Press, 1956.

Leaky, L.S.B. *The Southern Kikuyu Before 1903 Vols. 1-3*. London: Academic Press, 1977.

Kenyatta, J. *Facing Mt. Kenya*. New York: Vintage Books, 1965.

Muriuki, G. *A History of the Kikuyu, 1500-1900*. Nairobi: Oxford University Press, 1974.

CROSSING RIVERS

Made in the USA
Lexington, KY
25 August 2017